"Well, Quintus," the woman began. "Why have you come to be tested today?"

Silence fell like a blanket over the room. Quin traced the birthmark on his hand, knowing he had to be the one to speak first. He looked up at the examiners.

"Calling is in my blood," he said, trying to sound confident. From Davinia's snicker behind him, he hadn't quite succeeded.

"It is indeed," said the woman with another smile. "I doubt this will take long at all."

The man looked up. "We'll start with something simple," he said. "I'd like you to Call a banana."

Davinia snickered again, and Quin tried desperately not to think of how many times he hadn't been able to do exactly this.

This was it. Silence stretched out before them again. Quin felt his stomach turn and his head thump.

He knew he couldn't do it. He couldn't Call anything. And in about a minute everyone else was going to know it, too.

THE
CALLERS

THE
CALLERS

KIAH THOMAS

chronicle books · san francisco

Library of Congress Cataloging-in-Publication Data available.

ISBN 978-1-7972-1078-0

Manufactured in China.

Design by Lydia Ortiz.
Illustrations by Kaley McKean.
Typeset in Emblema, Lyon, and Lovelace.

10 9 8 7 6 5 4 3 2 1

Chronicle Books LLC
680 Second Street
San Francisco, California 94107

Chronicle Books—we see things differently. Become part
of our community at www.chroniclekids.com.

FOR LUKE.

CHAPTER ONE

Quintus Octavius had been staring at the same blank spot on the table for twenty-six minutes.

"Banana," he said, for the twelfth time.

He held his breath.

Nothing happened.

Again.

Quin opened his eyes as wide as he could. Maybe he wasn't staring hard enough.

Drops of liquid gathered at the corners of his eyes. His eyebrows ached.

"Banana," said Quin, a little louder this time.

His nose twitched. He opened his eyes even wider still. Something was about to happen; he could feel it.

Someone behind him snorted.

Quin froze. He hadn't realized there was anyone else in the room.

"I think you almost had it that time," said his sister, Davinia. Quin could hear the laughter in her voice.

He sighed. "What do you want, Dav?" he asked, keeping his gaze fixed on the table.

"I just want to help," she told him.

"I don't want your help," said Quin.

"Maybe you should try something else," said Davinia, ignoring him. She held out her hand. "Like an **orange**. Or a **melon**."

Quin watched as the air shimmered and the fruit thudded softly on the table.

Then Davinia held out her hand again. "Though a **banana** does sound good to me," she said with a sly grin.

But this time Quin was ready. He shot out his hand as the banana shimmered into being and caught it before it hit the table.

Davinia rolled her eyes as Quin pulled back the skin. "Nice one."

"Thanks," he said, with a confidence he didn't quite feel.

Quin took a bite, and Davinia's eyes narrowed again.

"You must be nervous about the test next week," she said.

Quin took another bite of the banana so he wouldn't have to answer and traced the leaf-shaped birthmark at the base of his palm.

"You know, I don't think there's ever been an Octavius who wasn't a Caller." Davinia grinned. "Just think, you could make history, little brother."

The first Octavius not to Call. In any other family, Quin's lack of ability would be normal. Callers were rare—the ability to Call, to conjure things, was a gift that appeared only once every few generations.

But in the Octavius family the ability was not exceptional. It was expected. And anything less than a strong Calling ability was not enough.

Quin felt a familiar twist in his stomach, the one that always appeared when he thought about the Octavius legacy and his failed Calling attempts. And the test was *next week*. He rubbed his palm again, then stopped when Davinia smirked at him.

"Shouldn't you be at Chambers?" said Quin, trying to shift her attention to something else.

Davinia's grin widened and Quin knew that she knew she'd gotten to him.

"Not today." She shrugged. "Council doesn't *officially* admit new members until after the tests."

Council, the ruling body of Elipsom, was based in their city, Orbis. It was made up of only the strongest Callers. New members were elected by current Council members.

Unofficially there was no way Davinia wouldn't be admitted. She was one of the strongest Callers to pass the test in the last five years. And she was an Octavius.

"Besides, what's more important than helping my little brother? **Chair**."

Quin almost jumped as wood hit the ground next to him. Davinia rested her hand along the carved back of the chair she had Called.

"You're not meant to Call constructed materials," he reminded his sister, even as he admired her skill. There was little point in reprimanding her—there wasn't much that Davinia took seriously. Quin marveled at the chair's smooth design and solid legs. It always amazed him how each Called thing seemed so unique.

Davinia raised her eyebrows. "And you're the expert?" she asked him. She watched him as he studied the chair. "What are you looking at?" she asked.

And because she did it without a bite in her voice, Quin took a chance.

"Do you . . ." He hesitated, trying to think of words that wouldn't make him sound as ignorant as he was. "Do you design the chair in your mind before you Call it?"

Davinia blinked, surprised by the question. She considered for a moment.

"No," she said. They both sat, the silence between them light for once, and Quin felt a flash of pride that he'd managed to ask a question about Calling that Dav hadn't considered.

"Others might have to, but I guess I'm just so good that it's instinctive," Davinia added, and the moment was gone.

Quin was working out how best to tell his sister to go away when a loud cry sounded outside the window.

They both looked up to see Dawn, their mother's rhinodrite, landing in their central courtyard.

"Mom's home," sang Davinia under her breath with a sideways look at her brother.

Quin ignored her, tracking Dawn's movements, his breath catching as it always did at the sight of her landing.

Like all rhinodrites, Dawn stood twice as tall as a human, and as long as three. With thick gray skin and horns like the common rhinoceros, rhinodrites boasted three major differences: their size, their loyalty, and a set of strong wings. Dawn's were currently stretched to capacity as she glided down.

Quin had always dreamed of riding one. Had *actually* dreamed about it more than once. Unfortunately, rhinodrites didn't tolerate the presence of anyone apart from the person who had Called them by name. Quin could still remember sneaking out of the house when he was younger to try and ride Dawn while his mother slept. Luckily, Adriana had woken in time to stop Quin before he got close enough for the rhinodrite to react. He could have been killed, she'd scolded him.

Quin hadn't tried again since, but sometimes he found himself wishing he was as bold now as he had been then. He still found it hard to draw his gaze away from the sight of the rhinodrite's power and grace.

Now, his mother was vaulting off Dawn and starting toward the house with long strides.

"I wonder if she'll be in a better mood," said Davinia, watching beside him. "She's been in a foul temper ever since her trip to the Spurges last week."

Not for the first time, Quin marveled at Davinia's ability to casually refer to their mother's mood, as if it wasn't terrifyingly unpredictable. He figured Davinia's confidence came from the fact that she didn't have to constantly try and prove herself.

She was right, though. Adriana had been in a bad mood since the Spurges.

The Spurges were just past the outskirts of Orbis. They were older than the capital city, and more derelict. The area was largely inhabited by people who refused to use or consume Called goods. They claimed that it was wrong to rely on things created from thin air. *Radicals*, Quin had heard his mother call them in her public addresses. *Wild* was what Davinia muttered to Quin whenever they were mentioned.

Quin still hadn't decided what he thought. All he knew was that people from the Spurges made him uncomfortable, with their passionate claims that nothing should come from nothing. The soil was as infertile there as it was on the rest of Elipsom, but they still insisted on growing their own food from seed. Generally, Council left them to their own devices. *They're too insignificant to bother*, his mother had said more than once.

Still, she'd bothered last week.

At the sound of his mother's footsteps, Quin pushed the thought aside. It wouldn't surprise him if she somehow managed to see into his brain.

"Are you sure you don't have somewhere else to be?" he asked Davinia as she sank into the chair next to him. "Like the other side of the planet?" he muttered under his breath. Though even from that barren wasteland, he imagined, Davinia would find some way to annoy him.

Davinia swung her legs up onto the table and leaned back.

"Nope," she said with a grin.

A moment later the door clicked open and Adriana Octavius walked in.

Quin held his breath and waited as she took in the items on the table, the chair, and Davinia lounging in it.

Her eyes sharpened on Quin.

"Who Called the fruit?" she asked. Not in a better mood, then.

Quin thought about lying, but she'd probably make him prove it anyway.

"Davinia," he said softly.

His mother was silent. She didn't even bother sighing.

"You shouldn't Call constructed materials," she said to Davinia instead, touching the back of the chair.

Though the words were a reprimand, Quin swallowed at the pride in her voice. Their mother might be Chief Councilor, but she was an Octavius first. Displays of power, particularly in her own household, always impressed her.

"Sorry, Mother," said Davinia, but she slid a look at Quin.

"Have you Called anything today?" his mother asked him. She already knew the answer. Quin suspected she just wanted him to admit it out loud.

"No," he said quietly.

There was a beat, and then, "Cassius has been making excellent progress with his Calling," Adriana said mildly.

Quin hated the feeling of shame that trickled through him. He was proud of his best friend, happy for him. But somehow the tone of his mother's voice alone managed to make Quin feel bad. He wasn't even sure how she knew about Cassius's Calling skill.

The room pulsed with silence again, and Quin's head hurt.

"A Council vehicle will collect us at nine tomorrow," said Adriana finally to Quin. "Don't be late."

She turned to Davinia. "Come, Davinia, I need your assistance with something," she said, before sweeping from the room. She didn't look at Quin again.

Davinia waved cheerily to Quin over her shoulder as she followed behind.

Where were they going at nine the next morning?

CHAPTER TWO

Quin was surrounded by green.

It wrapped around him in thick lines that twisted and darted away in every direction. He reached forward, and suddenly he was falling, breathing in color as patterns swirled around him.

Quin woke, a light sheen of sweat coating his forehead. His mouth felt dry.

He automatically fumbled for the notebook and pencils he kept beside his bed. His mind still half in his dream, he pressed pencil to paper, splashing patterns across the page until he felt like he could breathe again. Until the color faded from his mind.

He rested the notebook against his pillow as sunlight began to slant through his half-open window.

He'd been having the same dream for a few years now. Or a version of the same dream, at least. Two or three nights a week he would find himself ripped from a sleep filled with patterns so vivid he felt like he could touch them.

Quin flicked back through his notebook, studying the intricate patterns he'd drawn over the months before. They were all slightly different, he'd realized, but all related, like different pieces of the same jigsaw puzzle.

Maybe they were his brain's way of coping with his stress about Calling?

Quin looked up at his clock. There were still two hours before he had to get ready. With a sigh, he put his notebook back beside his bed.

His mother still hadn't told him where they were going, but facing it tired was unlikely to be a good idea.

Turning away from his notebook, Quin rolled over and closed his eyes again.

They were going to the Spurges.

Adriana had calmly announced it the moment they got into the sleek black car and then hadn't spoken again since. Reading her mood, Quin knew not to break the silence to ask why they were going. He watched out the window as they slid through the manicured streets of Orbis, blinking occasionally when the sun caught the wrong angle on a building and trying to figure out what his mother was up to. She hadn't asked Davinia to come, which meant she must have a specific reason for taking Quin.

They were almost on the outskirts of Orbis before she spoke again.

"You remember Milo Valerius," she said. It wasn't quite a question.

"I do," said Quin cautiously.

Milo had been in the same grade as Quin, up until his family pulled him out of class and moved to the Spurges. That had been the first time Quin had ever heard of someone moving out of Orbis.

No one had spoken about it after it had happened. Quin could even remember his mother firmly recommending he and Cass pick a new topic when she overheard them talking about it.

Quin hadn't sat at the same table as Milo, but he'd seen him every day. And then, suddenly, it was like he'd ceased to exist. Which, as Quin discovered when he researched it alone in the library later, he almost had. According to the one document Quin had managed to find, to move to the Spurges and willingly live a life without Called provisions, you had to request that your data be removed from Council's system. To give up your access to food supply and central medical services.

Most people who lived in the Spurges were born in the Spurges and died in the Spurges.

"Good," said Adriana, turning to face out the window again. He felt a thread of unease run through him. What did their visit have to do with his old classmate?

The vehicle hummed to a stop not long afterward, in front of a row of ramshackle houses.

"I am counting on your assistance today," his mother said, holding his gaze before opening the door and stepping out.

Quin felt the apprehension in his stomach pull into a knot. He wasn't sure whether the idea of his mother counting on him was better or worse than her silence.

The single-story house directly in front of them was an odd creation that might once have been all brick, but was now layered with a cobbled assortment of materials. Approaching, Quin could hear the faint sound of children shrieking and laughing.

He glanced at his mother. An almost invisible line of disgust wrinkled her nose.

They walked up uneven steps, past a large pot filled with small green buds. Quin ignored a sudden desire to touch the seedlings as his mother knocked on the door. Moments later it was thrown open by a woman wearing a clean apron over her tattered clothes. Her cheeks were flushed, her hair piled on top of her head, and she had a smile on her face that froze as she took them in.

She clearly knew who Adriana was.

"We are looking for Milo Valerius," said Adriana, her voice mild. Quin focused on keeping his breathing even. He smiled politely, but he could barely feel it touching his cheeks.

"Milo doesn't live here," said the woman bluntly, her eyes shifting between Quin and Adriana.

"Oh?" said Adriana. She raised her eyebrows slightly at the woman. "I must have been mistaken. Are you not Cecelia Valerius?"

On the surface the words were light. Quin wondered whether the other woman could hear the steel beneath them, and found himself hoping she could. He felt like they were speeding toward something, he just wasn't sure what—or how involved he was going to be in the crash.

The woman's eyes shuttered further, but she did not blink.

"I am," said the woman, her voice polite but firm. "But my son isn't here. He left home six months ago. I don't know where he is now."

"I see," said Adriana, picking a speck of dust from her sleeve. "Then you won't mind if we come inside?"

Cecelia didn't move immediately, her feet steady as she held Adriana's gaze. But even she must have decided the cost of defiance wouldn't be worth it. She swallowed, and stepped aside.

The inside of the house was sparse but warm. Quin kept his gaze focused on his mother's back. He hated feeling like he was intruding in someone's home.

"Have you ever read the Callers' Charter, Ms. Valerius?" asked Adriana, her voice dangerously casual. Cecelia remained silent, but Adriana wasn't really looking for a response anyway.

"It says that Callers are to be honored as they serve the community," she continued. "Of course, most Callers are delighted to Call for the good of the people. They are also bound to do so by law if such a gift manifests."

"Calling is a crime," said Cecelia, her voice soft. She kept her gaze forward, but Quin could see a muscle in her jaw twitch. Quin had never heard someone speak back to his mother. He felt a spark of admiration for this woman who would so fiercely defend her ideals— and her son.

"On the contrary," said Adriana. "Callers wasting their gift is the crime. Quite literally." She turned to face Quin.

"Quintus, I have a few questions to ask Ms. Valerius, but perhaps you might like to say hello to the other children outside?"

It wasn't a suggestion. This was where his assistance came in. She wanted him to find Milo. He felt sick.

Quin pushed open the back door to find himself in a yard that stretched beyond the house in either direction, a communal area shared among the entire row of houses.

Whatever game had been happening paused the moment Quin walked outside, and he found himself face-to-face with a group of twelve kids staring at him. A few were younger than him, looking confused about why the game had stopped. Most of the others were about Quin's age, studying him with fascination. And among them, Quin noticed with dread, there was a familiar boy with bright eyes and curly, dark hair.

"Milo." A smaller girl tugged on the boy's arm. "Your turn."

"Hush, Katya," Milo said softly, eyes on Quin. "We'll get back to the game in a moment."

"Who are you?" Katya asked Quin, looking up at him.

Quin offered the girl a small smile, but even that felt like a lie.

"I'm Quintus," he said.

"Do you want to play with us, Quintus?" asked Katya, and Quin's chest hurt at her openness.

"Why don't you all hide," Milo told her, "and I'll come looking in a minute."

Katya and the smaller children ran off. After a nod from Milo, a few older kids left as well, but most stayed close, shooting glances at Milo and Quin.

"It's nice to see you, Milo," said Quin. Because despite everything else, it *was* nice to see him. To know that he was okay. Happy, even.

"I wish I could say the same," said Milo. "Are you here with your mother?"

"She's inside," Quin answered quietly, rubbing his chest. Was he really going to point Milo out to her?

Milo seemed to be wondering the same thing. He eyed Quin warily.

"What's going on?" Quin asked. He had his suspicions, from what his mother had implied. But he needed to be sure. He couldn't just show her Milo without knowing why.

He wasn't sure Milo was going to answer him at first. But then the other boy sighed, and scuffed the dirt with his bare foot. "I never knew we had the Calling gene in our family. And one day . . . it's so stupid, I don't miss much from life in Orbis, but I missed strawberries." He rubbed a hand over his face. "I was describing the taste to some of the others, and when I said the word out loud . . . there was this power to it. A moment later, a strawberry appeared. Someone must have reported it."

He looked up again and met Quin's eyes.

Milo was a Caller. Which meant that he was legally bound to present himself to Council. Recruiting him was why they were here.

"You don't want to be a Caller?" asked Quin. His chest felt tight. His own life would be so much easier if he could Call, and Milo didn't even want it?

"I want to have a *choice*," said Milo desperately. "I hated it here at first. But it's different. I get to see things grow. To be part of a community that builds things."

"Calling could help this community, though," said Quin. "To move forward." He spoke the words, but looking behind Milo at the other kids . . . he felt the same divide in himself that he always felt when he thought about the Spurges. He found himself wishing he had Davinia's conviction that they were wild. From here, they just looked happy.

"Nothing good comes from nothing, Quin," said Milo, his face solemn.

Quin opened his mouth to answer, just as the door swung open behind him. Moments later, his mother and Cecelia appeared.

Cecelia's eyes flicked immediately to Quin and Milo, but she kept her face carefully blank.

She was breaking the law if she didn't give Milo up. And Quin was pretty sure everyone knew it. But without proof that Milo was Milo, Adriana couldn't remove him. There would be an uproar. Council's relationship with the Spurges was already on a knife's edge, and there was no way Adriana would risk a riot.

"Hello," said Adriana to Milo, her gaze flicking behind him to where the other kids were only half-hiding now, then back again. "I am Adriana."

"This is Zaccheus," said Cecelia quickly. "He lives next door."

There was silence, then Quin could hear his heart beating in his ears. This was the moment where he was supposed to jump in and correct her.

And yet Quin hesitated.

He didn't agree with Milo's choice. But he didn't want to be the one to take the choice away from him.

His stomach rolled as he thought about how quietly furious Adriana would be at being denied her goal. But if Quin didn't tell her, she wouldn't know. And without knowledge, she wouldn't act. Adriana Octavius was many things, but she was not impulsive. She valued control above all else.

Quin swallowed, and met Milo's eyes. He saw the fear there, and the resignation.

And he couldn't do it.

"It was nice to meet you, Zaccheus."

CHAPTER
THREE

He was on top of a ridge this time.

A breeze curled through his hair and danced across his nose, bringing with it the smell of rain and soil. Browns and greens stretched in an endless land-scape before him, flecked by the occasional speck of color. Quin looked down to see a steady stream of green weaving through the soil and pulsing beneath his feet. Instead of seeming strange, as he might have expected, the sight sent a jolt of warmth through him. He bent down to touch the ground, his palm pulsing in response, his fingertips tingling as the glow brightened. Patterns danced in front of his face, and Quin leaned closer . . .

Quin wrenched his eyes open, his heart still pumping to the beat of the imagined place.

He touched the sides of his bed, anchoring himself. It was getting harder to remember that the fresh soil and glow weren't real. He looked down at his hands, which still seemed to pulse with a phantom green. Quin brushed them on his sheets, as though by doing so he could rub it off.

He leaned back against his headboard, willing the cool metal to bring him back to himself. When it didn't give him what he needed, Quin pushed back against it and swung his feet to the floor.

The test was *today*. That thought pushed through the glow still clinging to the edges of his brain. Today was the day where it would be decided whether or not he was admitted to the esteemed rank of Caller.

What happened if he failed?

What happened when *he failed?*

Quin wasn't delusional—given that he'd never Called anything before, he knew that the likelihood of failure was high.

But he was an Octavius, and if there was even a slim chance that Calling ability would manifest under pressure, Quin had to take it.

As much as he'd rather stay in the place he'd apparently conjured in his head.

Quin shook out his arms and stretched his back.

He held out his hand.

KIAH THOMAS

He thought of Davinia's chair. Of her confidence.

He took a breath.

"Paper," he said half-heartedly. Nothing happened.

Quin sighed.

He pulled open the drawer and grabbed his notebook, determined to focus on the test.

He flicked past the early pages, ignoring the stab of dread and desire in his chest at the intricate green patterns etched on them.

Not today, Quin thought resolutely, flipping to a new, blank page.

What I know about Calling, he wrote.

He paused, pen tapping the paper.

1. **Calling is about intent. You have to want it.**

2. **Most Callers feel a tingle in the tips of their fingers just before an object manifests.**

3. **Calling is in your DNA. If you're not born a Caller, you will never be able to Call.**

Quin stared at the last item on his list. All Octaviuses in history were Callers. It *must* be in his DNA. That was just science.

He tapped the paper again, racking his brain for other facts about Calling. Unfortunately, despite the many shelves in the Orbis library dedicated to Calling records, there was nothing on how to Call when you simply didn't have the ability. Quin had looked.

He ripped the paper out and studied it. He should at least *try* to practice Calling again before the test.

With a glance back at point one, Quin tried to picture a banana. Even though Davinia had said she didn't design things before she Called them, surely it couldn't hurt.

He tried to *want* a banana. *A green banana, growing long, stretching in either direction, patterns dancing through* . . . Nope, no, that wasn't it. Quin shook the dream away from his brain. A *yellow* banana. With no glow. And no pattern.

"Banana," he said.

"Banana," he said again.

He focused as hard as he could, ignoring the faint smell of rain and soil that seemed to tickle his nose as the dream lingered.

"Banana!" he yelled.

When nothing appeared, Quin felt like banging the table. He tried it, just to see if it helped, then yelped when pain rushed through his hand.

"Idiot," Quin muttered to himself.

"Quintus." His mother's cool voice sounded through his door. "It's time to go."

Quin scrunched the paper into a ball and lobbed it into the trash. His mother would hate the idea of him writing down basic Calling concepts before the test.

She didn't come in though, and Quin quickly changed into his clothes. It was time.

They took a Council vehicle to Chambers. His mother sat in the front, her back straight, eyes fixed forward. Quin wondered if she missed riding Dawn. He would.

Davinia sat with Quin in the back. He could feel her eyes on him, but he kept his gaze fixed out the window; he didn't think he could take a battle with her today.

He watched the perfectly spaced trees along the sidewalk as the vehicle hummed past. Each was the same height, each neatly encased in a square box.

Quin thought back to the last time he'd driven past them, on the way to the Spurges the week before. A thread of guilt ran through him when he thought about the trip. His mother had been silently fuming when they returned home, but she hadn't questioned Quin. It would never cross her mind that he might have withheld information she wanted. Still, Quin couldn't help but wonder what Milo would be doing while Quin struggled through his test. Whether *he* would have any regrets.

Much too soon, they arrived at Chambers.

The building loomed in front of them, stretching across the entire block. Its shiny gray surface gleamed, dotted with windows in the same spacing as the trees on the sidewalk. Quin watched the reflection of their vehicle as it silently pulled to a stop out front.

As he often did, Quin wondered how often someone cleaned the exterior of the building. He had never been brave enough to ask his mother—or to lick the wall and see how long the mark remained. *Now is probably not the best time to try*, he thought as they exited the car. *Although it might provide a good distraction.*

He followed his mother into the building, stumbling slightly when he realized she was intending to use the main doors, even though they were steps away from the side entrance. Quin wasn't sure why he was surprised. Adriana Octavius was never one to make a subtle appearance.

To Quin's relief, once they'd passed through the main doors, the hallways were almost empty. He focused on breathing, listening to his footsteps bounce across the concrete floor and trying not to look at himself in the shiny walls. Davinia was unusually silent, for which Quin was thankful.

Still, when they entered the foyer leading to the Council rooms that served as testing chambers once a year, Quin would have sworn the whole room turned to look at them.

Quin's throat felt dry. He couldn't think about the other kids there to be tested. Doing his best to ignore the rising worry, Quin followed his mother to registration. She took a step back: far enough to give the illusion of independence, but close enough that she would still hear every word he said.

Quin cleared his throat.

"I'm here to be tested," he said.

The man at the counter barely looked up, keeping his eyes fixed on the screen in front of him and thrusting a metal pad in Quin's direction.

"Place your hand on this," he said. "So we can register your details."

Quin placed his hand on the pad, relieved that it wasn't shaking noticeably, and that the man hadn't looked up yet. It was nice to have a respite from people staring at him.

He focused on the coolness of the pad, let it steady him. A moment later there was a beep, and the man behind the counter jerked his head up. His eyes met Quin's, and then predictably flicked past him to Adriana. The man's face paled.

"Master Octavius," he stammered. "What a pleasure to have you with us today. Your testing will be in Room Three in ten minutes. If you'll just follow me, I can show you where to wait."

He stepped out from behind the counter and beckoned Quin forward, eyes flicking nervously to Adriana again as she and Davinia fell in behind them.

"Thank you for your help," Quin said quietly to the man, offering him a small smile. "I imagine you've had a long day."

The man smiled gratefully back at Quin before pausing, as though he'd finally worked up the courage to turn to Quin's mother.

"Ms. Octavius," he said, "I'm sure you know that it's protocol for candidates to be tested alone. You did write the charter after all, ha!" His eyes darted from Adriana to Davinia and back again.

"Of course I know, Marcellus," said Adriana.

The man looked shocked that Adriana knew his name. But Quin had a feeling he knew what was coming next. Adriana Octavius had not been elected Chief Councilor ten years running for nothing. Quin thought again of Milo's mother, of how impressive it was that she'd found the courage to stand up to Adriana.

"It is also in the charter that the Chief Councilor does what they need to keep themselves apprised of all Council activities," Adriana said. "This falls into that category."

Then, before Marcellus could open his mouth again, she stepped past him. "I'm sure you have other people awaiting your immediate attention," she said.

Quin's palms felt damp.

Was he really going to have to take the test with his mom watching?

CHAPTER FOUR

"Quin?"

A voice sounded behind them just as they arrived outside their room.

Quin turned around to see a boy with neat hair, immaculate clothes, and a wide grin looking back at him.

"Cass!" he said, feeling the pressure in his chest ease at the sight of his best friend. "How are you?"

"I'm really good," said Cassius, still grinning. He turned his gaze to include the rest of Quin's family. "Hi, Ms. Octavius, hi, Davinia."

"Hello, Cassius," said Adriana, and Davinia gave him a small smile.

Quin glanced behind Cassius to see an examiner step out of Testing Room 2.

"Have you just finished?" Quin asked his friend.

"I have!" Cassius's smile grew bigger, and Quin felt

an odd mix of joy and illness at the clear evidence on Cass's face that it had been a success.

"It went well?" he asked his friend quietly as his mother moved over to greet the examiner.

"It was great, Quin," said Cass. "I don't think I'm allowed to tell you much, but everything I Called came straightaway. I overheard one examiner say it was the best test he'd seen since, well, you know." He shot Davinia a small nod.

"That's fantastic," said Quin, meaning it. Cassius had never said so out loud, but Quin knew his greatest dream was to be a Caller and eventually to gain a seat on Council.

"You're up next?" said Cassius. "How are you feeling?"

Once, Quin might have told Cassius that he was dreading it. That he couldn't stop thinking about the moment when everyone would realize he was a failure.

But as Quin's Calling ability had remained non-existent and Cassius's had flourished, things had shifted between them slightly. They used to joke together about Quin's failed attempts. Now, any time Quin showed doubt or worry, Cassius looked at him with pity and discomfort. So Quin forced a smile to his own face.

"A little nervous," he said.

Cassius clapped his hand on Quin's shoulder. "We're both going to be Callers by the end of the day, I know it," he said. He turned back to Davinia and Adriana. "I should go and see Father, tell him how it went."

"Be sure to tell him that he should be very proud of you," Adriana said to Cassius.

Cassius flushed at her words.

"Thank you, Ms. Octavius," he said. "That means so much, coming from you."

The three of them watched as Cassius walked out through the foyer.

"He will make a fine Caller," said Adriana softly. But before Quin could respond, the door to Testing Room 3 slid open.

"Quintus Octavius?" a woman poked her head out the door. "Oh, Adriana, lovely to see you." She smiled at Quin's mother. "Are you all coming in?"

Quin felt his stomach sink into his feet as his mother and sister followed him into the room. Why were they coming too? Just to laugh at him? The door slid closed behind them, the soft click sealing them inside.

The room was empty except for a metal table where a man was already seated. The woman who had opened the door took her place beside him, then gestured for Quin to stand in front of them. Quin wondered for the first time what the rooms were normally used for, on a nontesting day.

"Well, Quintus," the woman began. "Why have you come to be tested today?"

Silence fell like a blanket over the room. Quin traced the birthmark on his hand, knowing he had to be the one to speak first. He looked up at the examiners.

"Calling is in my blood," he said, trying to sound confident. From Davinia's snicker behind him, he hadn't quite succeeded.

"It is indeed," said the woman with another smile. "I doubt this will take long at all."

The man looked up. "We'll start with something simple," he said. "I'd like you to Call a banana."

Davinia snickered again, and Quin tried desperately not to think of how many times he hadn't been able to do exactly this.

This was it. Silence stretched out before them again. Quin felt his stomach turn and his head thump.

He knew he couldn't do it. He couldn't Call anything. And in about a minute everyone else was going to know it, too.

The man tapped his fingers against the table. The woman leaned forward. Quin couldn't wait any longer.

"Banana," he croaked, feeling like his voice was scratching against the shining metal walls.

There was another beat of silence, and nothing happened.

The man and woman exchanged a glance. Quin's forehead felt hot and his palms were sticky now. They knew. They *knew*.

He stared at the wall, not sure quite what to do next. He wished he was anywhere else. He wished *this* was a dream he could wake up from.

The woman cleared her throat. When she spoke again, her voice was gentle. "I imagine you're feeling quite nervous today," she said. "Would you like to try again, dear?"

Quin looked up at her. She smiled kindly back at him. Try again? Quin felt a strange bubble of laughter build up in his throat. Excellent. That was just what he wanted. Another chance to prove that he couldn't do it.

But before he could decline, his mother spoke for him.

"Of course he would," said Adriana smoothly. Quin turned around to look at his mother, and she held his gaze. A smile touched her lips but stopped short of her eyes. Quin swallowed. There was no point in contradicting her wishes. She was Chief Councilor, so everyone in the room would defer to her. And if she didn't care that Quin looked like a fool, so be it.

"Yes, thank you," he told the examiner.

"Perhaps this time you could try an apple," said the man.

Quin focused on a blank spot on the table. He closed his eyes and tried to picture an apple. He tried to *want* an apple with every part of himself.

"Apple," he said, just as his mother coughed behind him.

But Quin barely noticed the sound.

Because an apple had just appeared in front of him.

"There's those Octavius genes," said the woman with a relieved chuckle.

Quin stared at the apple, then looked down at his fingers. Weren't they meant to be tingling? They weren't tingling.

He wasn't sure how he had expected Calling to feel, but it wasn't like that. The moment before the apple appeared, he hadn't felt anything apart from the usual frustration.

He thought about Milo and the strawberry. Maybe it was just a matter of wanting something badly enough.

Or maybe his stress had acted as a trigger, finally sparking his Calling ability to life.

Either way, he felt dizzy with confusion and relief.

"With speed like that, it's clear you're a Caller, but regulations say you have to Call three items," said the woman apologetically. She looked at the man, who consulted a screen on the table.

"This time, please Call wood," he said.

Quin was still shaking from his success with the apple. He couldn't quite believe it. He pictured a long, thin piece of wood, imagined it appearing in front of him . . .

"Wood," he said, just as Davinia scuffed her shoe on the ground behind him.

A short chunk of wood thudded into the room.

The woman grinned, and even the other examiner looked like he had relaxed a little. He leaned back in his chair, studying the piece of wood.

"Well done, Quintus," he said. He exchanged another glance with the woman, who inclined her head fractionally. "Finally, we'd like you to try Calling fire."

There was a small gasp from behind Quin.

"We wouldn't ask it in most tests," the woman explained, "but your speed with the last two items suggests that you might have the ability." She smiled encouragingly at him.

Quin wasn't quite sure what to think. Until that morning he hadn't been able to Call *anything*. Now he was supposed to be able to Call *fire*?

He focused on the space in front of him again, taking a deep breath and steadying himself. He doubted he'd be able to do it, but he had to try.

He tried to picture the wood burning, flames licking from its middle. He tried to imagine its heat, warming the room.

"Fire," he said.

This time, when his mother coughed, it was a beat too slow. The examiners didn't notice—they were too busy staring at the burning log in the middle of the room, wonder in their eyes.

But Quin heard it. The moment before the cough. The sound of his sister's voice, whispering the word along with him.

Fire.

He hadn't Called it into being at all. It was Davinia. All Davinia.

CHAPTER FIVE

"Congratulations, Quintus," his mother said as the room basked in the glow of the flames.

Quin jerked his head up and met her eyes, his chest aching. Saw the unspoken warning there.

Say nothing.

And so, even as he reeled, as his insides churned and his head thumped, Quin smiled graciously through the examiners' praise. Felt their joy like a punch in the gut and took the compliments that he did not really deserve.

He held the smile in place as they all laughed about his first attempt with the banana, and as Adriana led him and Davinia back past the testing chambers and down the hallways to the main entrance. He held it in place as he heard the snatched whispers that another Octavius had shown exceptional Calling ability, as he felt the eyes watching him all the way into the main foyer.

Quin clenched his hands and focused on the bite of fingers against palm as he put one foot in front of the other. Following his mother. Always, following his mother.

Their transport vehicle slid to the front of Chambers as they walked out of the building. Numbly, Quin opened the door for his mother and sister.

He stared out the window as they pulled away, unable to stand pretending a moment longer, but unwilling to face them yet. How long had they been planning it? Was saving face more important to them than the truth?

The worst part was, if Quin looked closely enough at himself, there was a small part of him that felt grateful that he wouldn't have to face down the public embarrassment.

Even now, his name was being added to the list of Callers. It would be officially announced at the end of the day. He wondered whether there was anything he could do to change it. Wondered what would happen if he marched into Chambers and declared that his mother had lied.

He knew. They'd never believe him over his mother.

"Well done, Quintus," his mother said finally.

Quin turned to look at her, hating the flush he could feel darting across his face.

"How long?" he whispered, unable to stop himself from asking for the details that kept tripping around in his head. Or to stop his voice from catching. "How long ago did you plan it?"

"We can clean and press your grandfather's robes," Adriana continued, as though he hadn't spoken. "You'll need them for the ceremony."

"I can't wear them," he said, shaking his head.

Adriana held his gaze, unblinking.

The robes were traditional. A vestige of a time long past when the first Callers had wanted to distinguish themselves from the masses. Now they were only worn for the induction ceremony. Most Callers chose to identify themselves via a simple wristband afterward. Privately, Quin had always thought that wearing the robes at all was ridiculous. Though he had craved it all the same.

"You are an Octavius," said Adriana softly. "And you will wear the robes of a Caller, as *all* your ancestors have before you."

Quin felt his protests die in his throat. He knew his mother. Knew that that was as much of an acknowledgment as she would ever give. And knew that once her mind was fixed, she wouldn't change it.

He glanced at Davinia, who hadn't spoken the entire trip. She looked out her own window, but Quin could tell that she was following the conversation intently. He wondered how she felt, helping her little brother to mark himself, falsely, as her equal.

And how was Quin supposed to maintain the facade of being a Caller? Was Davinia to spend the rest of their lives coughing and following him around?

Quin didn't doubt that their mother had a plan for that, too.

The transport vehicle drew silently to a stop in front of their house, and Adriana pushed open the door and stepped outside.

"We will, of course, celebrate tonight," she said to Quin, before nodding once to Davinia and walking inside, leaving silence again in her wake.

Davinia started to follow.

"Dav," said Quin before he could stop himself.

She turned back to look at him. Something Quin couldn't describe raced across her face before her features settled into a carefully blank expression.

"Please," said Quin, unable to stop his voice breaking on the word. He took a short breath and met his sister's gaze.

She stared back at him. "She first mentioned it months ago," she said finally, pushing his hand off her even as she gave him the information he wanted. "Though it wasn't confirmed until yesterday, when you still couldn't even Call a banana." She looked Quin up and down. "Caller," she scoffed, shaking her head. "Congratulations, brother." She slid out of the car and continued after Adriana.

Quin dragged his feet to his room, his mind numb as Davinia's words sat heavy on his skin.

He was going to be a Caller.

He pushed open his door and slumped down at his desk. He felt his eyes flick down to the trash almost automatically, like some part of him wanted to remember how foolish he'd been for even trying that morning.

But the scrunched-up list of Calling concepts wasn't there.

Quin felt his heart pause, then thump back into its usual rhythm.

What does it matter if she found it anyway, he thought bitterly, hearing the echo of his mother's steps down the hall. *She already knows I can't do it.*

Sitting down at his desk, Quin stared at his notebook until his vision blurred. He couldn't bring himself to open it, to see the pages from his dreams or the jagged line of the paper he'd torn out that morning.

He fumbled through his drawer for blank paper instead, needing to do something with his hands, even if he couldn't think what to write. He ran a hand across his face, embarrassed by the few tears that collected on his thumb and spilled down.

Then he pressed pen to paper and watched as the ink spread slowly outward.

He wished he knew why. Not why his mother had cheated the test—he was sure that was a matter of pride. But why he couldn't Call. He was an Octavius. Why was he the first one who couldn't do it? Why did people like Milo get the gift when they didn't want it?

If he wasn't a proper Caller, Quin had no idea who he was.

Rolling his pen away from the ink stain, Quin pressed harder, tracking letters along the paper.

Quintus Octavius.

False Caller. Dutiful son. Sucker. His mind filled in the blanks that, even in his current state, he wouldn't allow himself to write. He didn't need another piece of embarrassing paper for his mother to find.

He traced the letters of his name until paper started to rip across the Q, drops of liquid falling more quickly onto the paper now.

Quin pushed his chair back from the desk. He had no idea what to do next. Should he keep practicing? He dismissed the thought almost immediately. He wasn't a Caller. And maybe it was time to face that.

He rubbed his fingers along the mark on his palm and the memory of his dream caught in his throat. The warmth he'd felt there. A wave of longing ran through him. He felt like running screaming through the streets, or lying back on his bed and letting sleep claim him until after the official announcement. He wished he could recapture that sense of calm that came only during his dreams.

But he didn't do any of those things.

Because a moment later, the piece of paper he'd just written on disappeared as though it had been sucked into the air.

Quin pulled in a breath, rubbing his eyes. He must be going mad.

He ran his hand over the desk, pushing away everything else as he felt for the piece of paper. When the search was fruitless, he bent down to look on the floor, hoping it had somehow fallen down so quickly that he'd missed it.

It hadn't.

Maybe the piece of paper had never been there in the first place, Quin reasoned with himself. Maybe he had just imagined getting it out.

But when he looked at his hand, Quin could see tiny ink stains. He had written something. And now that something was gone.

It was like the opposite of Calling.

Quin almost snorted. That would be just the thing. To not only not be a Caller, but to make things *disappear* by accident.

He rubbed his eyes again, knowing that despite everything, he was probably going to have to tell his mother. Even if he couldn't bear the thought of being near her in that moment. Even if she thought he was imagining things.

But before Quin could do anything, a wave of nausea washed over him. He grabbed the desk in front of him, steadying himself.

His fingertips tingled. Then his arm. He blinked as his hands seemed to shift in and out of focus.

And then everything went black.

CHAPTER SIX

Quin woke to a pounding head and a heaving stomach.

What on Elipsom had just *happened*?

His hands ached behind his back. He twisted them, only to find they were stuck. The smell of damp hit his nose, and he felt his stomach roll again.

Why was there a smell of damp in his room?

Sucking a breath through his mouth and fighting down nausea, Quin opened his eyes.

He wasn't in his room.

Quin felt panic start to claw its way up his throat. How was he not in his room? He swallowed, forcing himself to breathe and look around. Freaking out wouldn't help anyone.

He was in a dimly lit cavern. Red-brown rock walls rose around him and soil shifted beneath his feet. From the corner of his eye, Quin could see a sliver of daylight where there seemed to be a passageway out.

And in front of him was a girl.

The girl was petite, with messy brown hair chopped short to her ears in a style Quin had never seen before. Her hand was clasped tightly around a piece of paper, slightly creased at the bottom. Hundreds of other pieces lay scattered on the floor around her. And she was staring at him in horror and fascination.

"Hello," Quin choked out. His throat felt like it was on fire.

The girl didn't answer. She backed away from him, paper crinkling beneath her feet.

It must be a dream. Quin used the thought to steady himself as he drew in ragged breaths. *I've just fallen asleep at my desk.*

They stared at each other for long moments.

"Who are you?" rasped Quin. "Where am I?"

"I'm Allie," said the girl. She narrowed her eyes, but didn't offer anything further.

Quin closed his eyes again. His head was spinning. He tried to move his hands again without success. Had she *tied him up*?

The material bit into his wrists, and the familiar desire to be a real Caller rushed through him, so he could Call a knife and slice through the bonds. But he had a strange feeling that a knife might not be enough. He'd never felt any rope like this material before.

He swallowed, fighting the almost overwhelming desire to just yell questions until he felt like he had even half an idea what was going on.

"Hello Allie," he forced out instead, striving to create some semblance of normality, even though the situation felt completely out of his control. "I'm Quintus."

"Quintus Octavius?" Allie whispered, staring in wonder at the paper in her hand.

Quin's ears rang as he followed her gaze. He could see the top of a *Q*. The tear stain on the bottom. She was holding the paper that had disappeared from his room.

"What?" He was embarrassed to hear that his voice was close to a shriek. "Where did you get that?" he ground out.

Allie froze at the unspoken confirmation in his response. Then, she dropped to the ground, desperately sorting through the papers on the floor.

"How is that possible?" she whispered to herself, hands frantic. "How is that *possible*?"

She looked up at him suddenly.

"You're from Elipsom?" she asked.

Before Quin could respond, a sound from the sliver of light in the rock drew both of their attention. Allie's head swung over, then back to Quin, eyes wide.

She scrambled toward him, thrusting her hand over his mouth.

"Don't say anything," she warned, but Quin could hear a thread of fear in her whispered command.

He thought about biting her hand, but . . . what was she talking about? Why would she ask if he was from Elipsom? Where was he, if not there?

The voices passed, and Allie met Quin's eyes, her hand still covering his mouth. Quin's head spun.

"Are you?" Allie asked again, removing her hand slowly. "From Elipsom?"

"Where else would I be from?!" said Quin, unable to stop the words bursting out of him. "And what just happened? Why am I even here? *How* am I even here? And where even *is* here?!"

Allie took a step back and started pacing the cave again, muttering to herself.

Quin took a breath, trying to clear his head. He needed information, and losing control wasn't likely to help him.

"What do you want from me?" he asked, more quietly this time.

Allie looked up again, determination steeling her frame. She seemed to have almost fully recovered from her earlier shock at seeing him. In some ways she looked as fierce as his mother, at three-quarters the size.

"You need to teach me about Calling," she said.

Quin's stomach dropped. He let out a bark of laughter, but there was no humor in it. *Of course.* He was tied up, in a cave, in a place he was pretty sure he'd never been in his life, and she was asking for the one thing he couldn't give. He hoped she hadn't kidnapped him based on the information that he was a Caller.

"Why are you laughing?" she demanded.

"You got the wrong Octavius," he told her, unable to stop the note of bitterness ringing through him. "I can't Call."

The words made Quin think of his mother, and icy shame washed over him. Did she know where Quin was? Was this all part of her plan?

He dismissed the thought almost immediately. If Adriana had organized it, Allie wouldn't be asking him to help her Call. And her reaction about him being from

Elipsom had seemed genuine. But then . . . where was he? And how had he gotten here? His mind kept going in circles.

Allie stormed toward him, "If you can't Call, then what is this?" she said fiercely, shaking the paper at him.

Quin's eyes swam as he took in the piece of paper. His notes on Calling. Why had she gone through his personal trash?

"Did you search my room?" he whispered.

"None of your business," Allie snapped.

"None of my business?" said Quin. "I *wrote* that, how can it not be my business?" He could feel hysteria rising in his voice, and he fought to push it down.

Allie glared at him. "You have no idea about ownership. You have *pillaged* this place. I am going to take back what is rightfully ours. And whether you can Call or not, you know *about* Calling. And you are going to help me."

Quin's head swam as he tried to follow. "What place?" he said. "I don't know what you're talking about." His throat ached and his wrists itched under the bonds.

Allie sighed, picking up a brown sphere that looked like it was made from bark. She shoved it toward him.

"It's just water," she said impatiently when Quin stared at her.

She shook it slightly so he could hear liquid splashing, then held it out to Quin again.

"Tip your head back," she said.

He didn't trust her, but he didn't see how she'd learn to Call by poisoning him. So Quin tipped his head back.

Despite its appearance, the rim of the container was cool and smooth. Quin felt immediate relief as the liquid hit his throat.

Allie took a breath, as though steadying herself.

"If you teach me what you know about Calling, I'll let you go," she said.

Quin looked around the cavern, pausing again on the light of the outdoors. If he could reach it, he might be able to figure out where he was. And how to get home.

Quin forced his gaze away from the gap, meeting her eyes. All he needed was a *moment*.

"Okay," he said slowly.

He could play along for now, and wait for an opportunity.

There was a long silence. "You want me to teach you here? Now?" Allie was looking at him expectantly.

"Do you have something better to do?" Allie raised her eyebrows at Quin as he twisted his hands again. The itch on his wrists was becoming a burn.

Quin didn't really see that he had a choice. At least she wouldn't learn much from him, anyway.

"What do you want me to start with?" he asked, thinking of all the books he'd read on Calling over the years.

She hesitated, and seemed to come to some sort of decision.

"Pretend I know nothing," she said finally.

Quin stared at her. Who *was* this girl? He'd never met anyone who knew *nothing* about Calling.

An odd sensation crept over him. What if he wasn't in Orbis anymore? Could he be in the Spurges?

Allie glared at him again, and Quin cleared his throat.

"To Call something is to will it into being," he began, pushing the words through his exhaustion and embarrassment. Teaching someone about Calling while tied up in a cave had to be the strangest thing he had ever done. He was still half expecting to wake up any moment now, though he knew in his gut that it wasn't a dream. "To conjure it from nothing."

Allie snorted. "Uh-huh," she said. "The truth, please, not more propaganda."

Quin frowned at her. "You asked me to start at the beginning," he said, his throat starting to give out again.

"Yeah, but I asked you to teach me, not spread lies," said Allie. She held the sphere of water out to Quin once more and he tipped his head to take another sip.

"I can't teach you if you don't let me." Quin gritted his teeth. It wouldn't help anything to get frustrated with her. He took a deep breath.

"Fine," said Allie. "Go on."

But before Quin could say anything else she jumped to her feet. "I should take notes," she said, picking her way through the paper on the floor.

"Is that my pencil, too?" muttered Quin, but Allie ignored him.

His wrists were still burning. He reached one of his fingers down to try and slide the cord-like material to a different spot. Maybe that would help.

But fire shot through his finger.

Allie looked back at him and Quin forced himself to hold still. The cord felt *looser*.

Twisting his hands again, a bolt of triumph surged through him. He was almost free!

With another wriggle, the cord came undone. Quin bit back a cry, just as Allie looked up again. He wasn't sure what she saw, but her eyes widened and she started to move across the cavern toward him.

Quin pushed to his feet, willing his legs to move.

She'd almost reached him. In other circumstances he might be able to overpower her. But his legs felt like they might give out from under him and his head was still throbbing. Besides, apart from tying him up, Allie hadn't done anything to hurt Quin, and he didn't want to hurt her. In desperation, he threw the cord as he started for the exit, hoping it might at least distract her.

A blinding flash of green burst through the cavern as it spun through the air. Quin halted, dazed. It seemed to have come from the *cord*.

But Quin didn't have time to stop and contemplate it. He stumbled, staggering, for the gap in the rock. Allie cried out behind him, in frustration or anger, he didn't know, and he squeezed himself through.

Only to come to a complete stop again.

Open space stretched out before him. Rich, brown earth that was interspersed with large patches of vivid green. Between the patches, plants pushed their way up through the soil at random. Wild. Free. In the distance

Quin could see the beginnings of a forest at the foot of a steep hill. And underneath it all, pulsing lines of green, weaving their way through the ground. This was *not* Elipsom.

But he knew where it was.

This was the place from his dreams.

CHAPTER
SEVEN

Quin sank slowly to the ground as dream and reality blurred together.

What was going on?

Allie burst out of the gap behind him, skidding to a stop when she realized that Quin wasn't running.

"Where am I?" he whispered again.

Quin could feel Allie's hesitation. And he wasn't sure what changed her mind, but a moment later she stepped up beside him.

"This is Evantra," she said, finally answering his question.

Evantra.

The word settled inside Quin as he watched the trees moving in the wind. The scent of damp soil filled his nose and stole through him, and Quin felt like weeping. An unexpected peace washed over him, even as his head was bursting. He could hear his heart beating in his ears, the pulse steady.

Cassius had once told Quin that there was something about the orderliness in Orbis that he found satisfying to his soul. Quin had laughed. He was pretty sure Cassius had been trying to suck up to his mother. But this, here—he finally understood what his friend had meant. Despite Quin's pounding head, there was something at the core of him that felt *right*.

He could sense Allie watching him, but his attention was held by the landscape before them, and the beauty in the disorder.

How had he dreamed of a place he had never been? A place he'd never even heard of? "What is this place?" he said finally, his voice hoarse.

Allie knelt down beside him. She paused, then rested a hand on his shoulder.

When Quin looked up at her she was studying his face.

Whatever she saw there, she made no move to tighten her grip, or to find a way to restrain him. It was like she knew how affected he was. Like she knew he was in no state to run away.

"You really don't know," she whispered, her eyes searching his.

"Know what?" said Quin. He'd take anything at this point.

Allie cleared her throat, her gaze drifting to the pinks and purples splashing across the sky.

"We can't talk properly here," she said, shaking her head and standing up. "It's getting too late." She looked back at Quin. "Will you come with me?" she asked, her voice hesitant.

Despite everything that was in his head, and everything that had come before, Quin laughed.

He stopped when Allie frowned at him.

"I don't really have a lot of options," he said.

"That's true," she said. But she held out her hand.

And even though Quin could barely think, even though he was struggling to breathe—there was something about it that steadied him. He took her hand.

They headed away from the cave, Quin following a step behind Allie. He couldn't look up without being overwhelmed, and so he focused on his breathing. On the next step.

He tracked the lines of green beneath the soil, twisting and branching out in front of him. He felt almost constantly compelled to touch the plants they passed. But the memory of falling through layers of green in his dream was vivid in his mind, and he kept his hands firmly by his sides. He tried not to notice how his heart seemed to beat to the strange pulse of the earth.

The sky grew dark around them, Allie quickening her pace as it did, and the background sounds began to shift. The rustling and low chatter of animals filtered toward them on the breeze, so different from the crisp silence he was used to.

"Why did you tie me up?" he asked Allie after a while. "Why was I unconscious?" The ground was rockier now, and began to slope upward.

Allie was quiet for long enough that Quin wasn't sure she would answer.

"It's complicated," she said finally. "More complicated than I can explain in a few sentences. But . . . Elipsom is not what you think it is. *Calling* is . . ."

She stopped abruptly, placing a hand on Quin's arm.

"What is it?" he asked, moving up beside her.

But a moment later it became clear why she'd stopped. A man and a woman in long robes appeared from around the corner ahead of them.

Were those *Callers' robes*?

Allie turned to look at Quin, her eyes bright with fear.

"We have to run," she said.

But for the first time in hours, Quin felt like he could contribute something. "It's okay," he said, stepping forward. "They're Callers."

There was a shout, and a bright-yellow light flashed.

A lumina ballista.

Lumina ballistas used targeted pulse waves to stun people and animals. The entire guard force on Elipsom carried them. On Quin's eleventh birthday, Adriana had taken him to watch a guard training session, and he'd tried using one. The power of the recoil had been enough to land Quin on his bottom. He could still remember the pain. And the expression on his mother's face.

What were *Callers* doing with lumina ballistas?

"Come on, Quintus," said Allie, tugging on his arm.

But Quin hesitated. If they were from Elipsom, they would know Adriana.

The thought of Quin's mother made his heart feel heavy in his chest. He wasn't sure he was ready to face her. Wasn't sure he wanted to go back, to accept a position he knew he didn't deserve. But he felt like it was his responsibility to get home if he could.

He rubbed his hand, wishing he had more time to think. Doubts clung to every part of him.

"They'll know my mother," he said quietly to Allie. "I can talk to them."

He was still too far off to see the Callers' faces properly, but he took a breath, then stepped forward with his hands raised. The Elipsom guards he knew wouldn't send a pulse on someone who was so clearly surrendering.

There was barely a pause before another yellow flash flew past him.

Quin froze.

Allie tugged on his arm again. "Quintus, we have to go," she hissed.

They'd sent a pulse wave on him. And even in his stupor, Quin realized he couldn't just stand there. *The Callers wouldn't help him get home.* The thought brought with it a sense of dread and wonder. He spun around to meet Allie's eyes. And then they ran.

Over soil and rocks they hurtled, the darkening sky flashing with yellow light.

Allie raced without stopping, guiding Quin between rocks and trees, avoiding open spaces where they could be easily targeted.

Because Callers were chasing them. But why would they be trying to stun two kids?

Allie looked back over her shoulder, then pointed to a dense thicket in front of a rock face before running abruptly toward it.

Quin sprinted after her. He wanted to tell her that hiding wasn't going to work. But he didn't know how long they could keep running, either.

They wove through trees, branches catching on Quin's arms. His stomach leaped into his throat as he realized that Allie was leading them straight for sheer rock. Adrenaline pushed him forward, the daze and numbness from earlier almost completely forgotten.

Allie ran straight up to the slab and Quin nearly stopped breathing, sure she would smack right into it, but then moments later, she was sliding *beneath* it, twisting into a gap between tree and rock.

Before he could think, Quin ducked in as well, breathing heavily as Allie slid the rock face back into place and locked them into darkness.

They held still as the guards approached. From behind the rock, Quin couldn't make out what they were saying.

The pulses weren't strong enough to shatter rock, Quin reminded himself.

But as the voices came closer, he could feel his heart thundering in his ears. Did they know where the gap was? Any moment now they could push back the rock and burst through.

Quin closed his eyes, waiting for the flash of yellow. His body tensed in anticipation and he could feel Allie holding her breath beside him.

They waited for a beat. And then another.

And then the voices started to move away again.

"Come on," Allie whispered. Quin stepped aside, expecting her to scramble back out again, but instead she turned and started forward into darkness.

He turned to follow and tripped almost immediately, not accustomed to the pitch-black.

"Here," Allie said, sliding her hand into his. Quin was sure he could hear a smile in her voice. He decided to ignore the idea that she might be laughing at him. "We're not far," she added.

The now-familiar smell of damp rose as they moved farther along what seemed to be a tunnel. Their path twisted downward, and before long Quin glimpsed a dull green glow up ahead.

Allie was walking briskly now. "You know where you're going?" Quin asked her.

The tunnel grew brighter as they neared the light, and Quin could make out the determined expression on Allie's face. It looked as though the light was coming from a cavern off to the side of the tunnel, and as they approached, Quin slowed his steps, readying himself to face whatever came next.

But Allie pressed forward, bypassing the entrance to the cavern. Quin twisted his head to look inside as they passed and was surprised to see a room full of color. Plants he'd never seen coated the wall and floor, and the whole room seemed to shine with a strange deep–green glow.

"Are those . . . ," Quin began, but Allie only pulled harder on his hand.

Not long afterward, they came to a dead end. Allie reached up and touched the top of the wall. Quin was half expecting it to slide open, and was surprised when a ladder fell down instead.

Allie swung onto the bottom rung, swiftly climbing to the ceiling. Quin wasn't sure what she was going to do when she got there.

She paused to look down at Quin, remnants of the green glow from the tunnel lighting her face.

"You're not scared of climbing, are you?" she called.

"I might be if you're leading," Quin muttered under his breath. He set his foot on the bottom rung and followed after her. When his hand was almost touching her foot, she reached up and pushed on the ceiling. Pale-green light flooded into the tunnel, and she moved up through the opening.

Quin took a breath. Then he pulled himself after her, out into the light.

CHAPTER EIGHT

"**A**llie!" Quin heard a man exclaim as he emerged into a room above the tunnels. "Where have you been? I was starting to worry."

It was a cavern, similar in size to the one he'd been tied up in earlier, but this one felt strangely homey.

Facing him was a small couch, and beside it were two tree stumps and a woven basket. Next to Quin was the open trapdoor they'd just come through, and a rug that looked as though it had been dislodged by their entry. The whole room was lit by three pale-green balls hanging from the ceiling. There was a doorway behind the couch, and another to Quin's right that seemed to lead further into the dwelling.

Allie stood in the center of the room, laughing as a man enveloped her in a hug.

"You worry too much, Dad," she said, but even Quin could hear the strain in her voice. His temples throbbed as he tried to keep up. Allie had been wary of the Callers as soon as she'd spotted them, but the chase seemed to have disturbed her, too. And she clearly didn't want this man—her father—to know about the incident.

"You've been gone all day . . ." The man's voice trailed off as he noticed Quin.

He took a step forward, positioning himself between Allie and Quin.

"Hello," he said, his voice steady but without any of the previous warmth. "Who are you?"

Quin straightened automatically, his years as Chief Councilor's son kicking in.

"My name is Quintus, sir."

The other man studied him.

"I am Marcus, Allie's father," he said finally. "Tell me, Quintus, where . . ."

But before Marcus could finish, Allie stepped out from behind him and placed a hand on his shoulder.

"Dad, can I talk to you in the kitchen?" she asked.

Marcus raised an eyebrow.

"I was just meeting Quintus," he said, sighing. He looked from Allie to Quin and back again. Then he started toward the door behind the couch.

"Two minutes, Allie," he called back to her, waiting at the doorway.

Allie glanced at Quin.

"Do you trust me?" she whispered.

Was she serious? "No," Quin whispered back. Allie grinned, the smile lighting up her face for a breath before she turned back to her father. Despite everything, Quin felt something spark inside him. He didn't know whether it was her smile or the freedom of answering without thinking. Maybe both.

She darted off to join her father, quickly turning back to look at Quin as they walked through the door and . . . did she *wink*?

He rubbed his head. They'd *left* him. He wasn't sure whether to be offended or complimented. He could run, he realized. Make his way back through the tunnels, figure out where he was, and find his way home. Part of him was tempted to.

But as he looked through the doorway to where he could see them standing, he knew that he wouldn't. Even after his hesitation with the guards earlier, Allie had stayed. She'd led him back to her home. He'd told her he didn't trust her, but by leaving him alone now, she was placing a piece of trust in him.

Even if he wasn't sure of much else, there was something in him that refused to betray that trust.

And he had questions.

He leaned against the wall as their voices floated through the cavern. He couldn't help but overhear them, though they weren't really trying to keep their voices down.

"No one sent him," he heard Allie say. "I know where he came from, and it's not Management. I promise."

Management? What on Elipsom was Management?

"Sometimes you can't know," said Marcus. "I don't need to tell you to think about what happened to your mother."

There was silence then.

"Quintus is different, Dad," he heard Allie say, and Quin felt his chest tighten at her automatic defense of him.

"Has Elipsom taken everything from him, too?" Marcus said, but Quin could hear the resignation in his voice. What were they talking about?

They came back through a moment later, and Quin pushed himself away from the wall. Allie grinned at him, and Quin raised his eyebrows, which only made her grin bigger.

Quin could sense Marcus watching their interaction, and he forced himself to meet the man's eyes.

"Allie has asked if you can stay tonight," said Marcus. "I said yes, but I would like you to know that I'll be sleeping here." He pointed to the couch. "There's no way out that's not past me."

"Yes, sir," said Quin. "I appreciate your hospitality."

"Come on," Allie said to Quin.

Quin started to follow her, but Marcus's words about losing everything kept tumbling around in his mind. He paused in the doorway.

"Really. Thank you for having me," he said softly to the man.

Marcus looked between Allie and Quin, then nodded once.

"I'll see you in the morning," was all he said in reply. But Quin was sure his voice was lighter.

They passed through what looked like a stone kitchen and into an even more sparsely furnished room. There was a tree stump in one corner, and a mattress in the other.

"I'm sorry," said Allie, her voice almost a whisper. "We lost my mother a few years ago." She stopped to face Quin. "And my dad, he . . . worries." Her voice caught, and Quin's chest ached for her.

"What was he talking about?" asked Quin. "What did he mean about Elipsom taking things?"

Allie stared at him for a moment, then sighed. "You should sit down," she said. She gestured to the mattress.

There was part of Quin that wanted to refuse, just to show that he could make his own decisions. But he wanted answers, and being petty wouldn't solve anything. Plus, he was exhausted.

Allie sat on the tree stump as he lowered himself to the mattress.

"What do you think is on the opposite side of the planet from Elipsom?" she asked. "It answers your question, I promise," she added when Quin gave her a look.

Whatever Quin had been expecting her to say, it wasn't that. "There's nothing on the other side of the planet," he said, feeling a little foolish. When Allie gave him a blank look he added, "You know, apart from the massive fields of ice."

Everyone knew that. There had even been an Exploration a hundred and fifty years before to confirm it. Still, there was something about the way she'd asked the question that sent a strange feeling creeping into the pit of Quin's stomach.

Allie's eyes flicked down to Quin's hand and he stopped tracing the mark on his palm.

"Why are you asking?" he asked, drawing her attention back to the conversation.

"Because that's where we are now," said Allie, holding his gaze. "On Evantra. The continent on the opposite side of the world to Elipsom."

Quin started shaking his head, even before she'd finished. His throat felt tight.

"That's impossible," he said. Because it was. "There's an entire wing of the museum in Orbis dedicated to the Exploration. It has images and soil and rock samples. There's no life on the other side of the planet apart from teekays, that species of snow mouse they discovered."

But even as he reassured himself, an errant thought snuck into Quin's head. *It could have been faked.* The idea seemed to take root, spreading itself through his brain.

Allie didn't say anything. She just sat there watching him, which was somehow worse than if she'd tried to convince him.

Quin swore he could feel the ground shift beneath him. "How could there be an entire continent on our world that no one knows about?" He could hear his voice rising, but he couldn't stop it.

Allie sighed. She rubbed her head, and for the first time Quin realized that she looked exhausted, too.

"I don't know," she said. When she looked up again her expression was unguarded, a mess of emotion on her face. Frustration. Uncertainty. Honesty. And there was something about seeing her messy and vulnerable that made Quin feel a little better—and a little worse. "Until I saw your reaction today . . . it didn't even occur to me that people on Elipsom didn't know about Evantra. I thought you were playing dumb in the cave," Allie continued. "There's communication between the two continents, so at least *someone* on Elipsom must know," she added when Quin raised his eyebrows at her.

Quin shook his head, needing to deny it somehow.

It couldn't be possible.

"I'm not saying I believe you," said Quin, to himself as much as to her, "but if what you say is true, how did I get here?"

Allie shifted on the stump.

"That's complicated," she answered.

"Try me," said Quin.

And even in the midst of the world shifting around him, he realized . . . he hadn't had such an honest conversation in years.

"You know how I was asking about Calling earlier?" said Allie.

"You mean when you had me tied up?" said Quin.

Allie frowned at him. "Yes," she acknowledged. She cleared her throat and took a breath.

"The thing is, I don't think you *know* what Calling is."

Quin opened his mouth—to protest or laugh, he wasn't sure—but before he could say anything, Allie continued quickly: "Hear me out. Please?"

Quin closed his mouth. He could do that. He nodded once. "Okay."

"A hundred and fifty years ago, a delegation set out from Elipsom," said Allie. "They wanted to discover what was beyond the seas."

"The Exploration," Quin confirmed.

"They found Evantra," Allie said, nodding. "It answered a lot of questions for them," she continued. "For as long as they could remember, some Elipsomians had been born with the ability to conjure things into being. It was a rare gift. Prized, and used sparingly. But in recent years they'd started relying on it more. After centuries of mining and building, the soil on Elipsom was becoming less and less fertile. So they had to make more and more things appear."

"Calling," whispered Quin into the pause.

"Calling," said Allie, taking a deep breath. "But when they discovered Evantra, they found a place where the opposite was true. A fertile land, plagued by an increasing number of disappearances."

She met Quin's eyes again. Quin's chest felt like it was pressing in on him.

"No one is quite sure what causes the phenomenon," said Allie. "But we do know this: What you term 'Calling' is not creating things from nothing. It is taking things from somewhere else. From . . . *here.*"

Quin closed his eyes, his ears roaring.

It couldn't be true. Because if it was true, Council had falsified the results of the Exploration. They'd rewritten history books. They had deceived hundreds of thousands of people. And if they knew . . . Quin felt bile in the back of his throat.

If they knew, it meant that they were willfully and systemically robbing an entire people.

"Why would the Evantrans go along with it?" he made himself ask, knowing that asking meant he was a step closer to accepting it as truth but needing the answer anyway.

"The first thing the delegation did was start to build a base here. One that would ensure Evantra continued to provide when things were Called. They promised our people that having a base would help stabilize the disappearances. They offered new tools and techniques—for agriculture, and medicine. They said that over time Elipsom's Council would gradually open up communication between the continents. That one day the relationship could be one of trade. That eventually, there would be no more disappearances." Allie sighed. "But by the time they'd finished building surveillance towers and it became clear that their promises were empty, it was too late. The Evantrans who protested were the first ones who disappeared."

"Disappeared?" asked Quin.

"It happens less now," said Allie. "Some Evantrans think the people who disappear are Called to Elipsom. To what fate, I don't know. But no one knows anything for sure." Pain flickered across her face and Quin wondered if that was what had happened to her mother.

He felt sick. She was talking about his people. *They'd* done this.

"How do you know?" asked Quin. His head was throbbing. How would he ever know what he believed anymore? Half of him wanted to simply dismiss what Allie was telling him. It would be easier to go on believing what he'd always known to be true. And who was this girl to tell him that every single thing about his life was a lie? What did she know?

"There was a man from Elipsom in the delegation that came," said Allie. "A Caller. When he found out what was happening, he refused to be part of it. He stayed on Evantra and he fell in love with an Evantran woman. And he had a family, who he told his side of the story. Who carried on his DNA."

She met Quin's eyes and held his gaze.

Quin stared at her, piecing together her words.

"You're a Caller," he said slowly. Which meant . . . she'd Called his paper. She'd Called *him*?

Calling a person was supposed to be impossible. But the nausea, the blacking out before he appeared on Evantra—it was like nothing he'd ever felt before. It had *felt* impossible. And how else would he have gotten here?

"Apparently so," said Allie. Her voice was light, but Quin could hear the tension and excitement in it. "We always knew the possibility was there, but there hasn't been one in my family since that first Elipsomian man." She exhaled.

Quin didn't know how to respond. He wasn't even sure how he was going to begin processing the information.

"Why are you telling me this?" he asked Allie. "And why should I trust you?"

Allie stood, stretching her limbs out.

"That's up to you," she said, not looking at him. "But I saw your face when you saw Evantra for the first time. Being here means something to you."

The room was silent. It was too much, all of it was too much. And yet, there was a pull Quin couldn't dismiss . . .

"Will you show it to me?" he asked, pushing the words past his pride.

Allie looked up. She nodded, and Quin felt something in him ease.

"Tomorrow," she said. "Tomorrow I'll show you everything."

CHAPTER NINE

Quin woke to sounds in the next cavern.

For a few glorious seconds he stared at the ceiling, ignoring the thoughts clamoring at the edges of his brain.

He had slept unexpectedly well. For the first time in a week his dreams felt steady rather than urgent, and he had woken slowly instead of being ripped from sleep.

Quin rubbed his head, still not quite able to believe that he was in a different place. Everything Allie had told him seemed impossible. And yet, as he turned it over in his mind, staring at the green bulbs on the ceiling . . . his gut told him that it was true.

Besides, the air here *tasted* different somehow.

Quin wasn't sure where that left him. He felt strangely disconnected from the information. Like his brain hadn't quite caught up yet. But beneath that, if he looked more closely . . . he could feel something burning in his stomach. Could taste acid in his mouth. Because if everything Allie said was true, then someone on Elipsom *must* know what Calling really was. And if anyone on Elipsom knew the truth about Calling—*his mother* most definitely knew. And yet she encouraged Calling. Mandated it, even. Why would she do that? Why hadn't she stopped it altogether?

The thought of his mother sent a current of panic through him. He wondered where she thought he was.

Quin traced his palm, which still seemed to be tingling from the bonds Allie had used. He had to work out what was happening, and what he was going to do. If he spent too long thinking about his family intentionally pillaging an entire continent for everything it was worth . . .

"You're awake!"

Quin looked over. Allie was standing in the doorway holding a pile of clothes.

"Good," she said, before he could answer. "We need to get going."

"Now?" said Quin, looking down at the blankets covering him.

"I need to show you," said Allie. "And I need to do it before the fields get too busy."

Quin pushed himself up to look at her. He didn't know what the fields were, but he figured he would find out soon enough.

"Fresh laundry?" he asked, gesturing to the pile in her hand.

"So you don't stand out too much," said Allie. She tossed the clothes to Quin and grinned when he caught them.

"Thank you," he said. Allie nodded.

"Come through when you're dressed," she said.

Quin shook his head as she left. She was bossier than Davinia. The thought caught him before he could stop it, and the acid in his throat rose. Did his *sister* know? He pushed the thought out of his head, then looked at the soft brown trousers and a cream shirt made from a thin material he didn't think he'd felt before.

Getting up and seeing the land would stop him from lying in bed going over the same information until it wore a hole in him. And he found that for all he was apprehensive about what he might learn, he was desperate to explore Evantra.

He pulled on the clothes and patted down his hair, which was sticking out at all sorts of strange angles. Then he took a breath and walked through into the next cavern.

Allie and Marcus were sitting together on the floor by the large tree stump that served as a table, murmuring to each other in low voices.

They stopped when Quin entered and looked up, Allie's gaze assessing and Marcus's slightly less sharp than it had been the previous day.

"Good morning," Quin said to Marcus.

"Good morning, Quintus." Marcus pushed a bowl toward Quin.

"Thank you," said Quin, slowly lowering himself down beside Allie.

In his bowl were small blue cubes and pink fronds. Quin cleared his throat. "I've never seen food like this," he said. "What is it? It looks wonderful."

"Evantran specialty," said Allie. "It's safe to eat," she added, just as he was about to take a bite. Marcus covered a smile when Quin paused.

Tentatively, Quin bit into one of the blue cubes. Flavor exploded on his tongue as it burst, like blueberries and watermelon all at once. He swallowed, warmth traveling through him. When the sensation passed, his mind felt clearer, more focused somehow.

Next he tried one of the fronds, and an unexpected smoothness ran down his throat, as though he was drinking a glass of cold milk.

What *was* this food?

He looked up at Allie and Marcus, but neither of them met his eyes, and Quin held his tongue. He was a guest in their home. Besides, it seemed like he would have plenty of time to ask Allie questions later.

Every mouthful was incredible, whatever the food was, but he ate quickly, trying to ignore Allie tapping the table as he did. As soon as Quin finished, she stood to her feet.

"Thank you for breakfast," said Quin, looking at Marcus. "You have a lovely home."

Years of making conversation as the son of a diplomat made the words feel trite, but Quin genuinely meant them. Despite Marcus's skepticism and all the strange furnishings, the cave felt more like a home than . . . his actual home.

"Thank you," said Marcus, his voice warm.

"I like the tree stumps," said Quin, resting his hand on the edge of the table.

"Luckily for us, tree stump seats aren't in high demand on Elipsom," Marcus replied, and Quin cursed his own thoughtlessness. If what Allie had told him about Calling *was* true . . .

"The disappearances *are* more predictable than they were historically," Marcus added after a moment, as though taking pity on him. "Since the delegation, every-thing is organized, at least. Less random disappearances from homes. But they haven't stopped completely. So the caves, the stumps—they're just safer choices." There was resignation in his voice, and Quin wondered what had gone missing over the years. He wondered if any of it was in *his* house.

He thought of Dav's chair.

He turned to see Allie watching him, her eyes curious. She held his gaze for a moment, then turned back to her father.

"We'll see you later today," she told him. "You'll cover for me at the fields?"

Marcus nodded. "Be careful," he said. He turned to Quin and hesitated. "Both of you."

An odd rush of warmth shot through Quin at his words, and he nodded to the older man, feeling strangely emotional. Marcus busied himself stacking the dishes.

"What did you tell him about me?" asked Quin quietly as they left.

Allie looked back at him. "Nothing," she said. "I just asked him to trust me."

She led Quin to another door, where the beginnings of daylight were starting to seep in, and Quin took a breath and steeled himself. But it didn't quite stop the beauty and familiarity of Evantra from hitting him in the gut when they emerged into it.

Morning light filtered through trees and danced over rocks. A thin mist hung over the horizon, and Quin could see droplets of water on the plants that sprang from the sides of the entrance to the cave. Quin's fingers itched. He wished he had his pencil, his notebook. The desire to sketch, to write—or even to just sit with the familiar comfort of pencil in hand—overwhelmed him.

Allie paused beside him.

"It still makes me feel like that, too," she said, so softly that Quin wondered whether he'd imagined it.

She started walking up a slope left of the cave, and Quin almost had to run to keep up. The ground beneath their feet was still, the green lines stark in the morning light.

Quin was about to ask Allie about the lines when they reached the top of the ridge. Patches of green spread out before them, like the ones Quin had seen the day before, but larger and more frequent.

In the distance he could see two large shapes moving around, and beyond them a gray tower rose above the green. Quin felt an uncomfortable twist in his chest at the sight.

"These are the fields," said Allie, keeping her voice low as they started walking down the other side of the ridge toward one of the large green patches.

"What's that?" Quin asked, pointing to the gray tower in the distance.

"Management," said Allie shortly, without looking up. "It's the Elipsom base," she added tersely in response to Quin's questioning look. "We'll go closer later, if we can."

As they neared the fields, Quin could see that there were rows and rows of fruit and vegetables hanging off vines and bursting from the ground.

"Is all this food for Evantra?" Quin asked quietly, somehow knowing in the pit of his stomach what her answer would be.

"Quite the opposite." She frowned. "The fields were set up to ensure there's a ready supply of crops available to be Called. And what is grown changes based on demand from Elipsom." Quin could hear the frustration in her voice. "Everyone on Evantra is required by law to work. Most people do it in these fields, though there are others who scout and plant new fields across the continent, and some work at Management. Everything for the good of Elipsom. There's even a furnace that we keep constantly burning in case anyone from Elipsom Calls fire."

"Last night you mentioned disappearances," said Quin, his voice careful. "Have there been many people who rebelled, over the years?" He could feel himself slipping deeper into Evantra with every question he asked.

Allie sighed, her gaze drifting to the tower.

"Every couple of years there's someone who challenges the system. Management is . . . quick to react. There hasn't been an outright war, if that's what you're asking. Management is too well equipped, and we haven't had the tools or the means to fight. Most people nowadays think we should be grateful that things are more ordered and less disappears unexpectedly."

Something about the way she spoke reminded him of the Spurges. Of Milo, who almost certainly didn't know the truth about Calling but believed in something passionately. Who stood for something. What did Quin stand for, apart from a desire to fulfill expectations? The thought didn't sit comfortably.

He cleared his throat and paused. "On Elipsom we have Calling Principles," he said, determined to contribute something to the conversation.

"What?" said Allie, stopping alongside him.

"Calling Principles," repeated Quin. "They're the guidelines that Callers operate by. Things they are and aren't allowed to Call, how regularly they're allowed to do it." They'd been invented to keep Evantra a secret, Quin realized, tasting acid at the back of his throat.

Allie was silent, considering.

"There was something like that on your piece of paper," she said.

"My paper?" said Quin.

"*What I know about Calling*," Allie recited. "It's how I Called you," she continued. She seemed more relaxed now that the conversation had shifted. Being out in the open suited her somehow. "I needed paper, and when I said that out loud, yours appeared."

The smell of strawberries filled the air as they passed a new set of crops. Quin breathed deeply, and the scent relaxed something in him.

"How did you get the other piece of paper?" Quin asked. Among the rest of the jumble in his mind, the circumstances of his arrival had been niggling at him. "The one with my name?"

"I was trying to get the rest of whoever's notes on Calling," said Allie. "You only had three points, and I thought there must be more, so I just kept Calling paper. When your name arrived, the writing looked similar, so I tried saying your name the same way I'd said 'paper.'"

Quin was torn between laughing and sobbing. What were the chances of her getting that second piece of paper? There were hundreds of thousands of other pieces that could have arrived.

"I Called paper for most of the day," she admitted, correctly reading his expression.

"All the material about Calling says that conjuring a person from nothing is impossible," said Quin. "It's illegal on Elipsom."

Something tugged at the back of Quin's head as he said the words, but when he tried to pull it into focus, it slipped out of his grasp again. He felt a surge of frustration, at all the things he didn't know, and stopped beside the field, taking a moment to breathe as he gazed through at the neat green plants bursting up in rows. Beside him was a vine, looping just above his head between wooden stakes. Quin could see fruit beginning to bud.

There was something about the line of it that steadied him, calmed his thoughts, and he reached up to touch one of the buds. He couldn't quite believe that they were the beginnings of something that would one day be Called.

His fingers brushed the side of the vine, and there was a sudden burst of green as searing pain flashed through his hand and into his chest.

Quin cried out, dropping his hold on the plant and staggering backward. Had something *bitten* him?

He closed his eyes against the wave of dizziness, then opened them to look down at his hand, bracing himself for it to be red or swollen.

Instead, the birthmark on his hand was glowing, pulsing with the same green light that moved beneath the ground.

Quin stopped breathing. He must be imagining it. He rubbed his eyes with his other hand, his throat tightening when the glow didn't disappear.

He looked up at Allie, who wasn't looking at him. She was staring at the plant.

Quin followed her gaze, his chest constricting.

A new tendril was pushing up out of the vine, and as Quin stared, a new fruit budded and expanded until it was as big as the others. As though it had always been there. As though four months had happened in a single instant.

"I knew it," Allie whispered.

CHAPTER TEN

"Knew what?" said Quin.

He felt like he was falling. "What just happened?" He stared at his hand, where the burning sensation was fading to a dull throb.

He looked at Allie, then back up at the vine, where the buds were now small passionfruit. "Did that just *grow*? While we were *watching*?" Quin rubbed his eyes again.

"It did," said Allie. There was something in her voice, a thread of excitement. She turned to Quin. "Do you have any idea what this means?"

"What?!" Quin asked, staring at her in disbelief. "How would I have any idea what it means?"

"I was hoping you'd be able to help me with Calling, but this is . . . a whole different thing." Allie studied the plant, lightly touching the new fruit. "We'll have to keep it to ourselves," she muttered. "I don't want to get anyone's hopes up."

"Are you going to tell me what's going on?" asked Quin, trying to keep his voice level.

He constantly felt like the ground was shifting beneath him, turning everything he knew on its head. In Orbis, he didn't have control, but there was a strange familiarity in the instability. He knew that there were things his mother wouldn't tell him. And there was always the hope of the library to retreat to, if he wanted answers, or his notebook, if he wanted solace. He knew the parameters of how everything worked.

Here? He had no idea what any of it meant.

Allie looked at him.

"Sorry," she said to Quin, and he could hear her excitement. The burning in his stomach rose at the sound. "It's just the first time there's been real possibilities," she said.

"Allie, will you *please* tell me what you're talking about?" The words burst out of him, his fear and frustration adding volume.

Allie swiveled her head around the field, searching, then back to Quin. "What are you doing?" she hissed. "Why are you yelling?"

And that was it. He snapped.

"Why am I yelling?" he shouted. "I passed a test I should have failed. I was Called to a place I had no idea existed, told that my people, my *family*, are stealing from the other side of the world. And I just touched a plant that made my hand feel like it was on fire and then it *grew a new fruit while I watched*. Wouldn't *you* be yelling?" Quin choked on the last words.

Allie just looked at him. "What was the test?"

But Quin couldn't take it. He felt like he was going to explode. He needed to get away, to be by himself.

"Give me a minute," he told Allie.

He turned and walked away, part of him registering that it was the first time he'd ever walked away from someone in anger, part of him all too aware of Allie following a pace behind.

So he ran.

He ran until his chest ached, and was glad of it, because at least this was an ache he could control.

The sky was getting brighter now, the sun lighting up the land as it rose. In the distance Quin could see figures emerging as the day began in earnest.

He kept running, knowing that it was probably stupid. Who cared? He didn't know where he was running to, but his hand was still throbbing. He was confused and frustrated and overwhelmed, but as the run burned away those things, there was also part of him that felt. . . anticipation. Like he was on the verge of discovering something about himself. Something wonderful. Something real.

He ran along the ridge, feeling the slight shift of soil beneath his feet, following the green lines, until somewhere along the way he stopped feeling like he was running away from something. Now he was sure he was running *toward* something. Like his body was being driven by instinct.

He stopped when the rocks beside him grew larger, bending forward and panting, his breath misting the cool morning air. Allie pulled to a stop beside him, and with grim satisfaction Quin noticed that she was struggling to breathe as well.

They stood for a moment, both recovering.

"Everything I have ever known is a lie," said Quin, finally admitting out loud the truth that had been building inside him since he'd arrived. "I didn't ask to be here. But I'm here now, and I want to understand. I need you to help me do that."

Allie nodded. "I'm sorry I didn't answer your questions," she said. "It's easy to get caught up." She studied

Quin, an openness to her face that he couldn't close himself off to.

"It's okay," said Quin. "Thank you."

She looked out over the fields, catching her breath.

"All my life, Evantra has existed to serve Elipsom," she said. "And every time there's hope that there might be another way, it dies." She looked at the tall tower, an almost imperceptible shudder running through her.

"I was nine when Mom disappeared," she said. "She had been collecting extra food from the fields to give to the families nearby who had more children under working age than they could feed. Management classed it as rebellion. They came to our house and they took her." She shook her head like she was shaking off the memory. "Sometimes I think our family carries the guilt of the Elipsom blood running in our veins."

She wiped her eyes, and Quin could see the anguish in them, and the fear that she fought to keep concealed. His heart hurt both for her loss and for her burden.

He didn't let himself think about his own mother, lurking in the shadow of his thoughts.

"Your hand . . . ," Allie said. "I think you are what we would call Vine-touched."

At Quin's look Allie sighed. "It is easier if I show you," she said. "Luckily you led us right where we need to be." She shot Quin a wry grin.

She pointed to the rocks beside them, then knelt down and reached underneath the side of one of the rocks. Quin heard a faint click and a moment later, the rock swung up. Another trapdoor. Quin swallowed, trying to temper the strange joy he could feel rising inside him.

"Can I go first?" he asked Allie, his heart thudding as his hand started tingling again.

Allie nodded, and Quin climbed inside.

There were a few steps of darkness and then he emerged into a tunnel that sparkled with green light, as though thousands of green gems had been embedded in the soil.

Without turning back to ask Allie, he headed toward the source of the light.

Moments later he came to an abrupt stop, his heart clenching in wonder at the open cavern before him. His breath caught.

The cavern was such a bright and vivid green that Quin could barely see. He shielded his face, the light on his hand dancing in response.

When his eyes adjusted, he saw that the room was almost entirely taken up by what looked like a massive, glowing tree trunk. Offshoots of green spilled out in every direction, wrapping their way around the walls and then disappearing into the soil. Through it all, green light rippled, so smooth that it looked like water. And something about the patterns . . . Quin felt a strange sense of déjà vu.

"What is this?" whispered Quin, unable to tear his gaze away.

"This is the Vine," Allie answered softly from beside him.

"A vine?" Quin half laughed in disbelief, unable to tear his gaze away from the rippling light. "This is not a vine."

"Not *a* vine," said Allie, and Quin heard the answering laughter in her voice. "*The* Vine."

"Like with a capital *V*?" asked Quin. He was partly talking to distract himself, he knew. To stop himself from pressing his hand against it and watching to see if green raced over him and through him.

"Like with a capital *V*," said Allie gently.

"Sure. Makes sense," Quin muttered, unable to stop himself from moving closer. His body screamed at him to touch it, to let himself be consumed by the green, but he held back. As he neared, he could see tiny black lines scoring parts of the trunk, as though the strands had been burned.

Allie came to stand beside him, touching one of the black lines.

"There are caverns like this across Evantra," said Allie. "Where you can access these trunks of the Vine. They're all interconnected. The Vine runs through the whole of the continent. A few years ago we noticed that some of the fields were yielding less than they used to—and some stopped growing things altogether. That's when we found the black strands. Every year there are more."

She turned to look at Quin.

"It's dying," she told him. "Some people think . . ." She took a breath. "They think that at one point the Vine ran through the entire planet. Until it died off on Elipsom hundreds of years ago. And if the current rate of Calling continues, if Evantra keeps having to provide for both continents . . . we're worried that it will die off here, too."

Somehow her words didn't come as a surprise. Still, Quin found he was overcome by a deep sense of mourning.

"What is Vine-touched?" he asked. He couldn't get the words out of his head.

"There are stories," said Allie hesitantly as Quin looked back to the Vine. "Of Evantrans over the years who were born with a special connection to the Vine. Who had the ability to make things grow at will. To cause plants to bear fruit and vegetables in an instant. In the stories, the Evantrans . . . they used offshoots of the Vine to make all sorts of new things. To mend things. And as they used it, the Vine drew strength from their interactions. Those interactions were what helped give it life and, in turn, it gave life to Evantra."

Quin kept his gaze fixed straight ahead.

"Those Evantrans were called Vine-touched," she whispered. Quin could feel her watching him.

She took a deep breath. "I haven't heard of anyone being Vine-touched in my lifetime. It's believed that the gene has faded out. And with Elipsom constantly taking things, and no Vine-touched people to help give the Vine life, we've feared that it will just slowly continue to die. Until Evantra becomes like Elipsom. And after that . . . what happens to the world?"

Quin closed his eyes, but even when he did, he could still see the Vine, glowing behind his eyelids.

"You think I can heal the Vine," said Quin, piecing together her earlier comments.

"I do," said Allie.

"I'm not from Evantra," said Quin. "How could I be Vine-touched?"

Allie hesitated. "I'm not sure. But I've never seen anyone do what you did with the plant just then."

Quin met her eyes. He needed time. He needed to think it all through.

"How long do we have here?" he asked Allie.

"I don't know," she said. "We should go before the fields get too busy."

They were silent as they made their way back through the tunnels. With every step Quin could feel the Vine pulling at him, drawing him back in. They stepped out into the open again. Quin blinked, his eyes adjusting to the shift in light. Even though it was still early in the day, the sunlight felt stark after the glow of the Vine.

He looked out at the fields to see that Allie had been right—there were already more people there than had been earlier.

A familiar cry pierced the air, and Quin jerked his head upward, scanning the sky.

A rhinodrite soared above them, wings extended, casting a silhouette across the land. The land seemed to shimmer as it flew across, the green tendrils stark against the soil. Quin felt a sense of calm steal over him at the sight.

"A rhinodrite," he whispered, watching as it landed on an empty field and three people slid down.

"You've seen one before?" asked Allie, watching him carefully.

Quin cleared his throat. "There are a few on Elip-som," he said, thinking of Dawn.

"Of course," said Allie, shaking her head. "That's why there are fewer than there used to be. I should have known."

"But . . . there were three people on it?" It was nice to think of something apart from the Vine he felt pulsing steadily beneath his feet.

Allie looked at him curiously. "What do you mean?"

"In Elipsom, only the strongest Callers can Call them," said Quin. "And they have to Call them by name—which is practically impossible. Once they do they are the only ones who the rhinodrite will allow near."

But as he spoke, Quin wondered at the truth of his words. Had his mother been lying about that, too? To maintain control?

He shook the questions aside, knowing there was little chance of him understanding the inner workings of his mother's plans.

"The rhinodrites are born with a connection to the land," said Allie as they both watched one of the men loop a rein around the rhinodrite's neck and begin leading it down the field. It kept its head down, horn digging deep into the soil. It was plowing, Quin realized. From where they stood he could see the ground beginning to shift, the glowing green moving closer to the surface. "The fewer rhinodrites there are, the less fertile the soil."

The other fields were getting busier, too. Quin could see people picking up tools and walking along the rows.

Quin's gaze drifted toward the row they'd walked past earlier. He wondered what had happened to the passionfruit he'd touched. Whether it had grown any bigger since they'd been underground.

"Any requests on where we go next, Quintus?" asked Allie lightly.

Her eyes twinkled, and Quin suspected she knew exactly which direction his feet were itching to go.

He met her eyes.

"Quin," he said, feeling something shift inside him. "Call me Quin."

CHAPTER ELEVEN

They kept their heads down, sticking to the side of the ridge to avoid attracting attention.

Quin could hear murmurs and soft laughter floating on the air as they passed the first field. It was strange to listen to people going about their day, and know that on the other side of the world people in Ellpsom were completely oblivious to the existence of an entire society. To know that he had been, just the day before.

His heart beat faster as they neared the field from earlier, and he quickened his pace. On one level he understood that his being Vine-touched was an impossibility, but on the other . . . he seemed to have grown a plant simply by touching it. Curiosity and nerves bubbled inside him at the thought of seeing it again—and confirming that he hadn't just imagined it.

He didn't know what to do with everything Allie had told him about the Vine. He felt torn between two places, two lives. Part of him felt like he should be trying to get back to Elipsom so he could see the other side of things. Maybe he could talk to people, let them know that Evantra existed. But how could he not stay and help, if he had the ability to?

He thought again about Milo, knowing so clearly what he wanted. Quin wished he had that certainty.

They drew closer to the field, and Quin realized there was a cluster of people gathered beside the plant he'd touched.

Allie came to a stop, motioning for Quin to do the same.

"We need to leave it alone," an older man was saying. "If we give it time, it may bear even more fruit, and we can figure out what is giving it life. These have *doubled* in size since yesterday. What could be causing that?"

"Just do your job," said the Caller who was with him. "Pick the fruit."

"Why would leaving it make a difference?" Quin whispered to Allie.

"It's impossible for something to be Called while it's still growing," Allie replied quietly. "Anything still attached remains untouched. I think it's about the disconnection from the Vine."

The crop had grown even more in the mere hour they'd been underground. Not much—but enough that fruit was clearly more abundant in one section.

"Surely it can't hurt to leave it for a day," a younger voice joined the conversation, and Quin saw a boy about his age step forward to stand beside the man.

"Are you questioning my orders?" The Caller's voice sliced through the air.

"I apologize, sir," said the boy, but even Quin could hear that he didn't mean it.

He could sense Allie's tension, and they crept closer to see that the older man and boy had positioned themselves in front of the plant. A girl stood just off to the side, looking up at the passionfruit.

The Caller tried again to move the man aside, but he refused to budge.

"Please," Quin could hear the man begging, desperation lacing his words. "You don't understand, this could . . ."

"I don't understand?" The Caller's voice was cold. "It seems to me that it is you who doesn't understand."

Quin felt Allie freeze beside him, and a sense of foreboding crept over him, even before she spoke.

"You need to get away from here," she said. "Now. Do you remember the way back?" Her eyes were bright with worry.

Allie started pushing him away, back in the direction of her cave.

Quin didn't want to be in the way, but he wouldn't just leave her if she was in danger.

"What are you going to do?" he asked, digging his heels in.

"I don't know," said Allie, her voice catching. "But once Demetrius gets passionate about something, he's hard to shift. I might be able to help."

"Let me help too," said Quin. "This was because of me. There must be something I can do."

Allie looked up at him, her eyes searching. Finally, she nodded, and started to turn back to the field.

Then they heard the Caller's voice rise.

Allie spun around, and a moment later a bright-yellow light flashed from the gray tower on the horizon, lighting the sky. Quin watched in horror as the old man and his companions crumpled to the ground.

The Caller stepped away from them.

"Pick this fruit," he directed the closest onlookers, before continuing on down the field.

Quin held his breath until the Caller was out of ear-shot. There was a strange ringing in his ears, and his head spun at the swift, violent resolution of the problem. He couldn't quite believe what had just happened.

"What was that?" he breathed, feeling Allie shake beside him.

"That was Management," she said. She turned away, and Quin could see her trying to steel herself. "They'll be okay," she said. It sounded as though she was reas-suring herself as much as Quin. "They're just stunned."

"What will happen to them?" asked Quin.

"Normally they're left there for the day and have to make up the time overnight. If they don't manage to pick their quota by morning, their family and their neighbors will miss out on food rations."

Quin thought of the Spurges, of Council encour-aging neighbors to report on each other. He could imagine his mother would like things like quotas. He felt sick.

Quin looked over at the people sprawled out on the ground. A few others had joined together to move their bodies into the shade.

"That's my fault," he said. "If I hadn't touched the plant it wouldn't have happened."

"No," said Allie fiercely, spinning to face him. "That is the fault of the man who chose to fire on them. Not you."

"Is there anything we can do?" Quin asked.

Allie shook her head, biting her lip. "Not without causing more problems," she said, her eyes shadowed. "Hopefully they'll wake by evening."

They made their way back to the cave. Allie was quiet for the first time since they'd set out that day.

He wondered how many times she'd seen the tower used. Whether she'd had that happen to *her*. He thought about the emotion in her voice whenever she described what was happening to her continent. And he felt like he might be starting to understand the thread of excitement in her voice whenever she spoke about Calling.

"Why do you want to Call things?" he asked her as they neared the top of the ridge that led to her cave.

Allie gazed into the distance. When she finally answered, her voice was soft. "Earlier this year, one of my friends was stunned by Management twice in one week. She still has a limp from the fall. And because she can't work as hard as she used to, her food allowance is lower. Last week, Demetrius cooked an anniversary dinner for his wife and half of it disappeared before they could eat it. Five years ago, my mother's favorite chair went missing. Do you see what I'm getting at?" Allie's eyes shone bright with unshed tears as she looked at him. "We have no control over any of it. We do what we can, but it is not enough. It is never enough. My father has spent my life hoping that I wasn't a Caller because he worries about what Management will do if they find out. I haven't even told him about it yet. But when I discovered that I am—I was glad of it. Because I am going to take back what is ours, Quin."

Quin felt his breathing catch at the passion in her voice. He cleared his throat. He couldn't stop thinking about the crumpled bodies at the edge of the field, and how helpless he'd felt when they'd fallen.

"Are there Callers at the fields at night?" he asked, an idea starting to form at the edge of his mind.

Allie frowned and shook her head. "They'll just leave a few tools for Demetrius, Louis, and Maya, then come back to check in the morning. If the work hasn't been done, or if they or any of the tools are missing, their family and neighbors will face the consequences."

Quin processed her words before taking a breath and making a decision.

"Have you Called anything apart from paper?" he asked tentatively. "And a person?"

Allie snorted. "I haven't had much free time since yesterday," she said, raising her eyebrows at him.

"The paper and me . . . we came from Elipsom," said Quin. "And even though Elipsom doesn't grow much, there are tools there. Gardening tools."

Quin couldn't believe he was suggesting stealing, but the tools were rarely used. They were unlikely to be missed.

Allie's eyes flew to Quin's. There was light sparking in hers, and he saw that she understood his meaning.

"From what I know, Calling is mostly about intent," said Quin. "I don't think you have any shortage of that."

Allie took a breath and nodded.

Quin smiled. "I'd start by holding out your hand."

CHAPTER TWELVE

They crept down to the field under the cover of darkness.

Between them they carried a bag filled with gardening equipment, which clinked every few steps until Allie Called some material to muffle the sound.

Out of caution, they had tried to avoid Calling too many tools. Though as Quin had said, it was unlikely such equipment would be missed. Most organic matter on Elipsom was Called rather than grown, so people rarely gardened seriously. Allie had looked deeply satisfied when the Calling worked, and though Quin felt her elation, he found himself silently apologizing to and thanking the original owners of the things they had taken. Then wondering whether the *original* owners were actually Evantrans, anyway.

The air felt crisp and the sounds of the evening floated on a gentle breeze. The sky overhead was clear of smog and clouds, the endless black pierced only by twinkling stars. Despite his nerves, Quin felt like he could breathe better than ever before.

As they neared the field, they saw a light where Demetrius and his companions had fallen.

Quin's eyes flicked to the tower again. They oversaw operations, Allie had explained. The one they could see was the main base, but towers just like it dotted the landscape across Evantra. And everywhere that wasn't covered by the towers' reach, there were patrols.

On Elipsom, the guard force kept a close watch on the Spurges, where riots occasionally broke out. But these towers were a whole new level of oppression, a permanent reminder that all Evantrans were under someone else's control.

The lines of green on the ground gave light to their journey, and before Quin could worry too much about how he would be received, they'd arrived at the field.

Demetrius and the others didn't notice them at first. They were working quietly, reaching up to twist passionfruit off one of the vines that ran across the rows.

Allie ducked under one of the plants, edging closer.

"Demetrius." She said his name softly, but the older man still jumped when he saw her.

"Allie," he said, stepping forward. "What are you doing here? I thought you were sick."

Allie shook her head and Quin realized that the field they were standing on was the one she normally worked on. The one she'd asked her father to cover for her that morning.

"I'm okay," she told Demetrius, without elaborating.

Sensing she wanted to avoid further questions, and feeling strange lurking in the darkness, Quin stepped up beside her.

"Hello," he said. "I'm Quin."

He decided to drop his usual formality the moment before he spoke, and he felt an odd rush of elation as the words left him. There was something liberating about introducing himself as Quin.

"Quin, this is Demetrius and his grandchildren, Maya and Louis," said Allie.

"Hello," said Louis, shaking Quin by the hand.

"Hi Quin." Maya smiled. "It's lovely to meet you."

"Nice to meet you, my boy. Where are you from?" asked Demetrius, clapping Quin on the back.

Allie shifted beside him, and Quin suspected there was every possibility she could make up a wild story if he let her jump in. They'd agreed not to mention Elipsom, but they hadn't decided on where they'd say Quin *was* from.

"My parents are scouts," he told the older man quickly. "We were on the other side of the continent until recently, setting up new fields. But I wanted to settle somewhere. To have somewhere more permanent to call home." He felt the words echo within him as he spoke, and turned to see Allie grinning up at him.

"Quin's my second cousin," Allie added, and Quin coughed.

Allie turned back to the others. "We've come to help," she said.

"Allie, no," said Demetrius, shaking his head. "Does your father know you're here?" He didn't wait for an answer before he continued. "You'll be exhausted in the morning if you do, it's not worth it. Besides, if they catch you helping, who knows what will happen."

He looked behind Allie to Quin. Unlike Marcus when he'd seen Quin the day before, Demetrius's face held no suspicion.

"It's really nice to meet you, Quin, and I appreciate you both coming down to help, but we're in for a long night. It is ours to bear, not yours." He shook his head.

"I still can't quite believe they picked it. Did you hear? Three extra passionfruit overnight. That's unheard of. If we'd left it, there might have been twenty by tomorrow. Something was happening to the Vine there, I can feel it. It could have held answers to the disease."

"I heard, Demetrius," said Allie softly. Quin held himself still, shoving his hands into his pockets. He didn't trust himself not to rub the mark on his hand. And although it seemed unlikely that anything would happen without him actually touching a plant, he didn't want to risk making the whole field glow by accident.

Allie held the bag out and gave it a shake. "We've even brought tools."

"Allie!" said Maya. "They'll know if some are missing!"

"Classic Allie," Louis muttered, then laughed at the look she shot him. Demetrius stepped forward and took the bag, a look of wonder on his face.

"I don't know how you do it, Allie, but you always manage to make an old man think he could have a heart attack at any moment. Where did you get these from?"

"You didn't break into Management again, did you?" asked Louis with a grin.

Quin shot a sideways look at Allie. *Again?*

"Someone needed medical supplies," she explained to Quin as Demetrius opened the bag. "Don't worry, we didn't break in," she told the others.

Demetrius pulled out a pair of pruning shears. "I've not seen any with these handles before," he said. "Where did you get them if not from Management?"

Allie just flashed Demetrius a grin.

"When have you ever known me to give away the best secrets, Demetrius?" she teased.

The older man shook his head and chuckled, the low sound making the others smile. "You will be the death of us all, Allie my girl. Or our salvation." The words were light, clearly in jest. But Quin saw the flash of anxiety that darted across Allie's face. She felt the weight of the words, no matter how they were said.

Quin stepped forward and took the bag from Demetrius, reaching inside. "I've not worked on, um, established fields for a while," he said, speaking the truth. "I might need some tips."

Demetrius shook his head. "I'd like a break from established fields. We can swap tips! You stick with me, Quin."

He rested a hand on Quin's shoulder, and Quin felt his eyes swim at the warmth of the weight. He shared a glance with Allie, and a sense of familiarity, of *belonging*, rushed through him.

The night passed relatively uneventfully. In the end, they spoke little, the silence punctuated occasionally by Louis trying to get someone to join him in song, or Demetrius calling everyone over to study a particular crop. They harvested the fruits and vegetables in large baskets that Allie had told him would be taken to Management.

Quin was careful not to let any of his bare skin touch a plant. Still, his whole body pulsed with energy, and the plants around him seemed to grow gradually brighter.

Between the five of them, they managed to complete the work they'd been assigned while the stars were still bright in the sky.

Demetrius grasped Quin by the hand, his fingers crushing Quin's.

"I can't thank you enough for your help," he said hoarsely, his voice clogged with emotion. "There is nothing quite like our community. And this girl, our Allie. She is the heart of it. Just like her mother." He released Quin's hand.

Out of the corner of his eye, Quin saw Allie duck her head at the words.

"I really enjoyed it," said Quin honestly. "Truly," he added when Allie raised her eyebrows at him. Demetrius beamed.

"Our rations are in short supply at home," said Louis, grinning at them both. "Would you two be interested in a trip to the Garden? I heard the new crop of maengober-ries is flourishing!"

Allie froze, her eyes shooting in Quin's direction.

Demetrius noticed her look. "Does Quin not know about the Garden?" he said, his face falling. "We just assumed, since he's your cousin . . ."

"*Second* cousin," said Quin softly, nudging a smile out of Allie.

"No, it's okay," she said, shaking off their concerns. "Quin has been to the Garden. He just hasn't had maengoberries yet. I've been eating them too quickly for him to get a taste."

She grinned and the others visibly relaxed, before collecting their things and making their way out of the field.

Quin touched Allie's arm.

"Maengoberries?" he whispered.

She searched his eyes with hers.

"Please promise me you'll keep this a secret?" she said as the others pulled ahead.

It was a tone he hadn't heard her use.

"The Callers don't know about this garden?" he asked.

She shook her head. "And they can't, Quin. It's the only consistent food some people here have."

Quin didn't even need to think about it. "I promise."

Allie smiled at him.

"Are you guys okay?" Louis called to them over his shoulder, and they hurried to catch up.

They entered through another trapdoor, emerging almost immediately into a glowing green section of tunnel that Quin recognized. It was the one he and Allie had taken the day before.

A sense of excitement spread through his chest as he realized they were right near the room full of color that Allie had rushed him past. Quin could *feel* it, like the energy was pulsing out of the room through the Vine.

The others were waiting at the entrance, the same smiles on their faces that Quin could feel starting to pull at the edges of his mouth.

He hurried forward, Allie right beside him.

As he'd glimpsed the day before, the room was bursting with color. Plants hung from every available space, richly loaded with food Quin had never seen. Aware of Louis, Maya, and Demetrius, he did his best not to stare. Red, purple, and white flowers covered one side of the floor, with thin paths weaving through the flowers to allow access to the rest of the cavern. The other side of the floor was taken up by at least ten different shades of green. From the ceiling, large pink fronds hung, and Quin wondered if that was what he'd had in his breakfast. He followed Allie, dazed, until she stopped at a bush of red flowers. She snapped two off and passed one to Quin, gesturing for him to take a bite. Quin did, only to find it was unexpectedly salty, like pretzels. He felt a giddiness he hadn't felt in years; he couldn't believe how happy it made him just to be in this room.

In the back corner, long, yellow sticks clumped together to form a bush taller than Quin. Allie pulled a bundle of the sticks out.

"Welcome to the Garden," she whispered to Quin with a grin. "Hold out your hand."

When he did, she broke the end off one of the sticks and then tipped it sideways, small, squishy, red and yellow balls tumbling out the end.

"Whoa," he said.

"Maengoberries," said Allie, pouring some into her own hand and popping them in her mouth.

Quin followed suit, the balls exploding with sweetness in his mouth. They tasted like the freshest mango he'd ever eaten, dipped in ice cream. He grinned back at Allie.

They made their way back over to the others, where Louis was organizing a pile of food.

Allie handed a few maengoberry sticks to him, and he broke the end off one and tipped out a pile of berries. Laughing, he tossed one to Maya, who caught it in her mouth.

"Allie!" called Louis when she leaned down to add the food she and Quin had collected to the pile.

"No fair!" she laughed as Louis tossed one berry in the air at her, and then another. She missed the first, and caught the second in her hand before throwing it straight at Quin.

Quin turned his head quickly, opening his mouth and catching the berry with a grin. He swallowed, a trickle of ice-cream flavor running down his throat.

Maya laughed and clapped. "Quin's on my team next time we play ball!" she called as Louis wrapped an arm around Quin's shoulders.

Demetrius joined them again, some greenery and three blue bulbs in his arms.

"Not the brocini," groaned Maya.

"It's good for you." Demetrius winked at Quin. "Can't just eat the sweet stuff." He walked over to Louis to help him get the food ready.

"Your grandfather is fantastic," Quin said to Maya.

Maya stuck her tongue out, but her eyes were twinkling as she watched her family.

"Have you both been working down here with Marcus this week?" she asked Quin and Allie, smiling at them both.

The Garden, Louis had called it earlier. Quin looked around the room again. Beneath the crops, thick ropes of green Vine ran around the walls and through the soil. A secret, life-filled garden. A food source, with plants he had never seen. *If people on Elipsom didn't know about them, didn't know the names of them, they couldn't Call them*, he realized.

"Felt a bit mean to put Quin to work straightaway," said Allie after a quick glance at Quin. "Maybe next week though."

"It's wonderful down here," he said truthfully.

"It's a special place." Maya smiled back at him. "You fit right in. And I'm sure Grandpa will rope you into helping with the Garden in no time, if you have any skill with growing at all. Even if you don't."

"Are you coming?" Louis called from the other side of the cave.

Maya skipped off to her brother, and Allie grinned at Quin.

"Race you," she said.

And as he matched her grin and raced ahead, Quin found himself wondering: *Could he stay on Evantra?*

CHAPTER
THIRTEEN

They sat on the ground, food spread before them.

"I'll get the bowlates," said Allie, jumping up and ducking into a small nook beside the cavern.

What in the world were *bowlates*?

Demetrius smiled fondly after her.

"Always sees what needs to be done before everyone else, our Allie," he said. "I still remember the day she came to me with the idea for this place." He shook his head at the memory. "I thought she was mad. 'Let's make it so that no one has to go hungry,' she said."

"Allie made all this?" said Quin, looking around the cavern. "It's incredible."

"No," said Allie, reemerging with small, smooth baskets that looked like they'd been made from tightly woven cord. "I just had an idea. The Garden was created by everyone."

Allie handed a basket to each person, hesitating slightly before she placed one before Quin. *Bowlates*, she'd called them. Not bowls, or plates. *So they can't be Called either.*

There was no polite order as they started loading the food into the bowlates, everyone taking and giving and jostling over the pink fronds. Louis and Maya broke into a heated debate about how much brocini they *had* to eat.

"Bowlates?" laughed Quin softly to Allie.

Allie rolled her eyes. "Someone said it as a joke," she said, "and then it kind of just stuck. Once or twice someone has tried naming them something else, but we always end up back at bowlates."

Quin leaned forward to inspect one more closely, marveling at the pattern of the weave.

"Don't touch them, though," Allie warned him, resting a hand on his arm. Could his Vine-touch unravel a bowlate completely? He kept his hand away just in case.

Demetrius looked over at them. Allie waved her piece of brocini at him.

"I don't think I told you that Demetrius is the head gardener down here. And he is brilliant."

Demetrius smiled. "My grandmother was Vine-touched," he confided to Quin. "Not that I am myself, but sometimes I like to think that maybe I got a drop of the gene. Two years ago this place was nothing more than seeds. Makes you wonder whether the Vine knows what we need, and helps us along."

Quin felt a nervous excitement at the mention of the Vine. "You've done an amazing job," he said. "Especially with the brocini," he added, taking a bite of the blue bulb. Warmth pulsed through him when Demetrius laughed and Maya groaned.

There was an easy silence, and Quin glanced at Allie, who was piling more food into her bowlate. *Two years ago.* From what Allie had told him, that must have been not long after her mother had been taken for stealing rations for other people. And even though Allie was clearly deeply affected by it, her response hadn't been to give up, but to create a way forward.

He wondered again at her role in the group. The others clearly regarded her with affection and respect. But when they'd worked in the field Quin had noticed that they seemed to defer to her as well. Like she was their leader.

"So what are the outskirts of Evantra like, Quin?" asked Louis, helping himself to another serving of the blue cubes. "Is the land still fertile out there?"

Demetrius leaned in closer to hear Quin's response, accidentally knocking over his bowlate as he did. Food spilled out the side, and Quin automatically reached out to steady it before he heard Allie squeak in warning.

There was a bright flash as the green in the cavern pulsed brighter. Around them, the plants, fruits, and vegetables seemed to grow brighter, too.

Quin felt his heart sink as he looked down at the bowlate, now shining with a faint green light where he'd touched it. His fingers tingled. He could feel the weight of the others' gaze on him as silence fell.

He steeled himself, then looked up to meet their eyes.

Louis's mouth was wide with shock, a blue cube forgotten in one hand. Maya had a small smile on her face, looking between Allie and Quin.

And Demetrius . . . Demetrius had tears pooling in his eyes.

"My boy," he said. "Oh, my dear boy." He reached out to clasp Quin by the hand. "Never in my lifetime . . . I can't even imagine . . ." He seemed unable to finish a sentence, and Quin found that he wasn't sure how to start one himself.

"The bowlates are made from the Vine," said Allie, and Quin felt an unexpected burst of humor at her wry tone.

"Yeah, I got that," he said to her, and something in him lifted when she half smiled back at him. Maybe this wasn't going to be a disaster.

"You're Vine-touched?" said Maya, giving life to the words that sat in the space between them.

Quin looked over at Allie, but she was silent, letting him answer the question himself.

"I'm not sure," he answered honestly. "Maybe. But . . ." He looked to Allie again, inviting her into his answer. Telling them too much would reveal Allie's secret as well. And no matter what he did, she had to continue living with these people, with the weight of their expectations.

Maya caught the look between them. "It's okay," she broke in softly. "It is enough for us to know this spark of hope. I know any details might compromise your safety."

Louis, mouth finally closed, nodded his agreement. He rubbed his hands together in a gesture reminiscent of his grandfather.

"Can you show us something?" he asked eagerly.

A tremor of unease passed through Quin at their hopeful expressions. His shoulders began to ache with heaviness, both draining and warm.

"He's still learning," said Allie, jumping in quickly. "It might be too soon." Quin looked up at her in surprise, his chest warming as she sent him a small smile. She didn't stand to benefit from protecting him, but she was anyway. It was that compassion and understanding more than anything that made him nod.

"It's still new," he said, "but I can try." Allie's expression barely changed, but Quin saw the shift in her eyes. The hope that lit in them. He swallowed. "And I'm not sure where to start."

Louis grinned, and Maya clapped as Demetrius gripped Quin's hand harder.

Demetrius jumped to his feet, wiping his eyes.

"There's a new crop that I haven't been able to figure out yet," he said. "Would you . . . could we try something with that?"

Quin nodded, and the others followed them to the side of the cavern. On the edge, behind a massive bush of pink fruit, were two small shoots.

"I've crossbred two different species, trying to make something similar to the pink fronds," said Demetrius, frowning as he studied the plants. "But for some reason they aren't growing as quickly as I would like."

Quin knelt down beside Demetrius, feeling a little foolish. He hesitated, then stretched out a hand to touch one of the plants. Almost immediately, a faint glow lit the leaves, like an echo of the light of the giant trunk they'd seen earlier.

The others were silent behind him as Quin held the edge of the leaf. But apart from the green glow, nothing happened. No new fruit burst forth; the plant didn't start growing. Quin began to sweat, the feeling reminding him horribly of the Calling test. He couldn't do it.

He heard Demetrius shift beside him, and Quin took a breath, and then another. And he turned his mind away from Elipsom, to Evantra. To where he was. To his decision to help Allie when she'd asked, to help the others in the fields. Those were his decisions. And even if he failed at this—at least that would be his, too. There was no one here to pretend for him.

He focused more carefully on the plant, running his mind along the leaves and down the stem, letting himself be absorbed by it. He could see the path of green in his mind, and as his mental exploration went lower, into the roots, Quin realized what the problem was. With a breath, he took hold of the roots with his mind, imagining them running deeper into the soil and closer to the Vine.

When he was satisfied that it was done, he reached out to the other plant and repeated the process.

Finally, he pulled back to himself, and looked up to see the others gazing at the plants. Unbelievably, there were already changes taking place. The pink was brighter and a few small green buds had appeared at the tips of the stems.

Demetrius was staring at Quin in wonder.

"It looks brighter. And it . . . *feels* healthier," he said. "I'm not sure what it is, but I can sense the difference in it. What did you do?"

Quin swallowed, his throat dry. He felt a little like he might collapse, and leaned into the hand on his shoulder. Louis passed him a bark bottle like the one Allie had given him yesterday. Quin drank gratefully, swallowing again before he answered.

"The roots were shallow," he told Demetrius. "It seemed like they needed to be closer to the Vine so . . . I pulled them together. I think," he finished weakly, unable to think of a better way to describe what he'd done.

"Incredible," whispered Demetrius. There was a happy silence as they stood around the plants.

"We should go," said Allie finally, studying Quin's face. "And try and get some rest before morning."

Quin nodded and let them help him to his feet.

Louis clasped his hand, and Maya hugged him.

"It has been an honor to work alongside you," said Demetrius solemnly. "I'm looking forward to getting to know you better, Quin. And not just because you are Vine-touched." He winked and clapped Quin on the back.

They left soon after, Quin and Allie walking quietly back to the trapdoor to her cave. Quin tried to sort through the weight of emotion that hung heavy on his shoulders.

He *liked* the Evantrans. Their resilience, their ingenuity. He liked Allie, despite the circumstances of his arrival.

If he didn't try and help, the Vine might die. And that would be disastrous—not only for the people on Evantra and their secret food source, but possibly for Elipsom as well. What happened on Evantra affected Elipsom.

And after what he'd just done—he'd fixed that plant!— he didn't know if he could walk away.

He might try to help and watch it die anyway—he knew that.

But Quin found that he couldn't just sit back and let it happen.

"I don't know if I can make a difference," he said aloud to Allie. "But the Vine . . . I'll do whatever I can to save it."

CHAPTER
FOURTEEN

They chose a cavern close to Allie and Marcus's home to access the Vine.

Quin had thought about asking Demetrius for help, but despite his knowledge and experience, something about having him there made the possibility of failure seem too real.

He'd told Allie he didn't need her there either, but that hadn't stuck. She'd been so determined to go with him that she'd eaten a rotten piece of brocini and hobbled down to the field to prove to the overseer that she was sick. Quin woke up when she arrived back, her cheeks drawn and eyes determined, her rations docked for three days.

Despite thinking it was a little excessive, he was glad he'd have her with him.

In theory, testing the connection could have been done anywhere, but the giant, glowing trunks of Vine underground seemed like the most obvious place to start. Quin could almost feel them reverberating beneath the soil.

They set out after breakfast, Marcus going so far as to shake Quin's hand before they left.

"She's happier, with you here," he said quietly to Quin when Allie told them she just needed a moment to sit.

"Maybe not right now." Quin grinned.

Marcus looked over at Allie and chuckled. Allie glared at them both from her position on the couch, then pushed determinedly to her feet.

"You told your dad about me being Vine-touched?" Quin asked as they left the cave. She'd asked if he was okay with her telling her father the day before.

Allie nodded.

"What about your Calling?" Quin asked more cautiously.

"Not yet," she sighed.

The gene was passed down through Allie's mother's family, so Marcus must have known it was possible. But since so many generations had passed with no Callers, it seemed unlikely that one would be born.

Quin wondered what his own mother was doing. He wondered what she was thinking. Where she thought he was. Would she just assume that Quin had run away after his failure in the test? Part of him hoped so. He didn't know what she'd do if she discovered what had actually happened.

He forced the questions from his mind as he sensed they were nearing the cavern that held the trunk.

Thinking of the passionfruit situation, they had decided to avoid the cavern they'd already been to in case something Quin did affected the fields.

The cavern was slightly smaller than the last one, and the bright-green light when they stepped inside was less of a shock than it had been the first time. Quin traced the leaf shape on his palm, blinking when the light in the cavern seemed to flicker in response. Anticipation hummed through him, chased by the realization: He didn't actually know where to start.

"How do I . . . what do I do?" he asked Allie.

"No idea," said Allie. "I figured you would just sense it. Like you did yesterday."

He wasn't really sure why he was surprised by the response. He'd noticed that Allie often did things before she'd really thought about them.

Although she was right this time—he *had* just sensed it the day before.

Taking a breath, he stepped toward the Vine, then before he could overthink it, he reached forward and rested his hand against the glowing trunk.

It was like the small crop and *nothing* like the small crop all at once. Where the day before Quin had had a measure of control, had been able to guide his thoughts, today he had none.

Green light shot through him, pouring into him until it was all he could see. Ice chased heat across his skin, lit up his veins, and sent pain throbbing through his body. He was on the brink of exploding, even as a sense of wholeness shot through him.

He saw the Vine and was *inside* the Vine all at once. He saw the patterns running through it, layers upon layers of intricacy that he hadn't seen from outside. He saw the streaks of black that stretched longer and deeper than he had imagined. And even as he was over-whelmed, a spark of memory tugged at Quin. Something in the patterns within the layers that he recognized. That he'd seen before.

He tried to grab hold of the thought, but lost it in the sea of green, too powerful for him to direct.

He saw—he felt—trees and plants and flowers and soil. Roots and vines and death.

All in the space of a moment.

He yanked his hand from the Vine, unable to bear it.

At the loss of contact, the blinding green faded. The pain ebbed and his vision started to clear.

Quin sank slowly to the ground, resting his head in his hands. He felt the loss keenly, like something had been wrenched from within him.

Allie knelt down beside him, hesitating before placing a hand on his back. She didn't flinch at the touch, though Quin felt like his back was on fire.

"What happened?" she asked after a moment.

"I don't know," said Quin, voice hoarse. "It was like I was inside it, like I could feel everything that was connected to it."

He flexed his fingers and traced the leaf shape on his palm again, waiting for his heart to slow. For his body to feel like his own again.

"There were patterns," he said at last. "Layers to the Vine." He looked to the glowing trunk, trying to see past the smoothness of the exterior. "You can't see them from here, but . . . I'm sure that I've seen them before." He searched his mind, trying to find the right thread of memory to tug on.

He closed his eyes to block out everything else, and suddenly he saw himself standing atop a ridge, green lines weaving before him.

"My notebook," he whispered.

"Your what?" said Allie.

"My notebook," said Quin, his voice stronger. "I use it to sketch and to write and I . . ." He hesitated. Somehow, despite everything, it seemed a strangely personal thing to share. He cleared his throat.

"I dreamed about Evantra," he told her. "The view from the top of the ridge, out over the fields—I saw that. And then there were other dreams, with green lines and patterns that seemed to fill every part of me, they were so vivid. I drew them. Those dreams, those sketches . . . they started a few years ago." He looked over at the Vine, then back at Allie. "Around when you said the black streaks started appearing here."

"You think . . . you think the dreams began because the Vine was dying?"

Quin nodded. "And I'm pretty sure they're the layers *inside* the Vine."

"Do you have the notebook with you?" asked Allie.

"It's in my room," said Quin. "On Elipsom."

He met Allie's eyes, realization dawning on him. "You could Call it," he said.

Allie looked thoughtful. "It took me a long time to get the right paper, but I can try."

She held out her hand almost immediately.

"**Notebook**," she said.

A bright-pink, sparkling book appeared in front of her.

Quin laughed, feeling some of the tension drain out of him. He picked up the notebook, touching the cover.

"Not this one," he told her with a grin, which faded as he wondered who it had been taken from—and whether there was any way to return it. He thought again of all the things that had been taken from Evantra. And this, seeing something that so clearly belonged to someone else . . . it hit home how personal it was. And how irreversible.

"Any ideas?" Allie asked, pulling him back to the moment at hand.

Quin tried to remember if he'd heard or read anything that might help. Davinia had said she didn't picture things when she Called, but maybe that was because she never Called something she'd heard described.

"Maybe try picturing it," Quin said. "It's black. And faded. Slightly bigger than my hand. Oh! It has a Q the size of my thumb in the center."

Allie took a breath, closed her eyes, and held out her hand again.

"**Notebook**," she said firmly.

There was a beat, and then they both gasped as a small black book shimmered and thudded to the ground in front of her.

CHAPTER FIFTEEN

Quin picked it up, running his hand over the familiar cover.

"It worked," he whispered. "I can't believe it worked."

He looked up at Allie, grinning back at him.

Quin took a breath, then opened the cover.

It was everything Quin had just seen, on paper. Page after page, each a different layer. Without knowing what it was, or what it meant, Quin had dreamed and drawn a breakdown of the Vine. And for all that it was disconcerting, there was something oddly comforting about the realization. He ran his fingers along a page, memorizing the way the lines wove together.

Allie came to sit beside him, and Quin flipped through the book, showing her the patterns, until he came to the jagged edge where he'd torn out the page with his Calling notes. He touched it, marveling at the fact that he'd done that only two days ago.

"I think I might be able to fix it," said Quin slowly, a wave of nerves washing over him as he spoke the words aloud.

He could feel Allie tense beside him, but she didn't speak, didn't rush him.

"It's all the pieces of the Vine that I just saw. If I go slowly, and maybe talk to Demetrius . . . he could take me to the places where the Vine is dying. And the notebook will help me figure out what I need to do." He looked up at Allie, and at the hope in her eyes, he felt compelled to admit, "I'm not sure it'll work, though. I may have made things grow, but those things were already alive. Those black scorch marks . . ." He shook his head. "They aren't. I can't tell what to do with them."

Allie stared at him for a moment. She reached into her pocket and pulled out a length of cord. The one that had tied Quin's hands. It lay flat and lifeless in her palms.

"It's an offshoot of the Vine that was cut long ago," she said, turning it over in her hands. "When you touched it, Quin, you made it glow. If anyone can do this, it's you."

She held the cord out to Quin. He stared at it, breathing slowly through his nose before putting his notebook on the ground, then reaching out and taking it from her.

The effect was immediate.

The piece of vine grew steadily greener, but after the shock of his connection with the trunk, the strangeness of the sensation barely registered. He was getting used to the feeling now, he realized. Quin focused on his hands. He didn't have a particular plan or direction. He would have to *sense* it, he thought wryly, feeling a wave of triumph that, at last, he could remain calm while touching it.

He thought about what it felt like to pull the roots down the day before, and this time he pictured the piece in his hand growing longer. He concentrated, seeing new shoots in his mind. He heard Allie gasp as slowly, slowly, a speck of bright green started pushing its way up out of the vine and taking shape.

Buoyed by his success, Quin concentrated harder, imagining the brocini Maya and Louis had so disliked. He remembered the taste of it on his lips, the face Maya had pulled when she'd taken a bite. He imagined what its roots might be like. Quin poured the sensations and memories into the cord of vine in his hands, used it to weave the Vine together. The new shoot began to harden, and as he watched, it gradually changed color from green to blue.

"Is that . . . ?" Allie's voice broke Quin's concentration, and he lost his hold on the thread that seemed to be tying him to the vine in his hands. The brocini shrank back into the vine, but the new shoot remained.

"Brocini." Quin grinned, elation flooding through him as he came fully back to himself. "I think if I'd grown it more fully it might have stayed."

Allie blinked at the vine, then looked up at Quin. Then, before he knew what was happening, she'd thrown her arms around him.

Quin's face heated at the emotion, and he hesitated before hugging her back. It had been so long since anyone had hugged him at all—and never like that. He felt the warmth flood through the rest of him as he held her.

"It still might not work with the living Vine," he said, but he couldn't stop smiling as he shoved the cord into his pocket when Allie finally broke away. The thought of the entire Vine still overwhelmed him, and he hadn't really achieved anything, but this . . . this felt like hope.

"We'll get there," said Allie, quickly dashing her tears away. "Maybe I can Call something that will help." She cleared her throat. "I think we should stop for today, though," she said. "This is amazing."

She smiled at him, and Quin smiled back. He couldn't quite believe how different he could feel in a day.

He picked up his notebook and they made their way back through the tunnels, an easy and companionable silence falling between them.

Quin opened his mouth to ask whether they could pass by the Garden and pick some maengoberries when he felt it.

A strange tugging sensation. Pulling at his feet and his hands and his chest.

It wasn't the Vine. It was . . . *no.*

It felt like last time, but different, too. Then, it had tingled and he had slipped into unconsciousness. This time it was like his insides were being twisted and yanked.

Quin gasped, and Allie stopped walking. She turned to look at him.

"Quin?" said Allie, her voice confused. "Are you okay?"

"Allie," he said, his voice thin. "I think . . ."

But he didn't get to finish his sentence. Because a moment later, it was as though his body was being ripped apart.

And for the second time in his life, everything went black.

CHAPTER SIXTEEN

Every part of Quin's body was aching as he woke. He gradually became aware of a softness at his back, and a clean, slightly metallic scent in the air.

No.

He was back in his room. Back in Elipsom. *Not now!*

He kept his eyes closed, as though by doing so he could shut out the smell and feel of Elipsom. Could pretend that his other senses were deceiving him.

Then, a wave of nausea washed over him, the same feeling as when he'd first been Called to Evantra, and Quin felt a surge of relief. *Allie was Calling him back.* She had realized what had happened, and she was Calling him back. .

His fingertips started tingling, and he quickly felt around for his notebook. He'd been holding it when he was ripped from Evantra, and he'd need it for the Vine.

But it wasn't there.

It doesn't matter, Quin reassured himself as his arms started tingling as well. Allie could Call it again.

There was a sigh from next to him.

Quin froze, stilling his hand. He wasn't alone.

"**Quintus Octavius**," said a soft voice, and Quin felt himself jolt back into the present, the nausea fading abruptly, the tingling suddenly ceasing.

Heart aching, Quin swallowed and let his eyelids slowly flicker open. His mother came into focus. She was sitting beside the bed, watching him.

She Called me, Quin realized, weight settling in his stomach at everything that the realization confirmed. She had pulled him back from Evantra, which meant that she knew about Evantra.

And from what he could tell, she'd just Called his name again. Was she *holding him* on Elipsom?

How much did she know?

"How are you?" she asked, leaning toward him. "I'm very pleased to see you awake. It's been a long few days, and we've all been quite concerned about you."

Quin met her eyes, his spine prickling at the coldness in them. He let his gaze slide past her, out his window.

From where he lay he could see empty, dull-blue sky. He felt like he was going to be sick.

"I'm fine," he said quietly.

"You've been unwell, Quintus," said Adriana, her voice even. Quin gripped the edge of his bed. He would not let her see him react. He looked over to his desk and his chest tightened as he saw the familiar black book that lay there.

Was she seriously expecting him to believe that he'd been in bed since the day of the test? Or was she just assuming that he'd play along?

Quin breathed slowly. There had been a tiny part of him hoping that he'd been wrong, he realized. That his mother had somehow not known what was happening. But he couldn't lie to himself any longer.

He reached down to touch the vine in his pocket, to steady himself, only to realize that it was missing as well. And . . . he was back in his own clothes.

His mother had *changed* his clothes. And his notebook was on the desk, but *where was the vine?* How long had he been unconscious? Anger burned in his stomach. He hated that Elipsom and his mother made him feel so immediately off-balance again. One moment he'd been on Evantra, with a place and a purpose, and the next he was lying helpless in his bed.

He looked at his mother to see her already studying him. He had to say something.

Quin cleared his throat.

"I'm sorry to worry you," he said, the words tasting like dust in his mouth.

"You've been very unwell," his mother repeated. "You'll need some time to recover." She leaned forward again and touched Quin's forehead. A tremor ran through his body, and he held as still as he could to stop from flinching.

"You were talking quite a bit in your sleep," she said. "Were you dreaming?" Her tone was a blatant attempt to sound casual. Quin had never heard her speak like that before.

"I'm not sure," Quin lied. "My dreams never make much sense, though." His mother held his gaze, then smoothed the side of his hair. He stayed frozen, trying to remember the last time she'd tucked him into bed.

"Never mind," she said. "Rest, now. We can talk more when you're well."

Despite his aching body, Quin didn't feel tired. But he closed his eyes anyway. He wasn't sure how long his mother sat, but he didn't hear her leave.

Eventually he fell asleep.

❋❋❋

When Quin woke again it was to find Cassius sitting beside him, staring into the distance.

Quin felt himself relax slightly into the mattress.

"Cass," he croaked, voice rough from sleep.

Cassius looked over at him, his face breaking into a grin.

"Quin! Adriana said you'd woken, but I had to see for myself."

Quin felt the room spin around him and braced himself against the nausea. His heart beat faster as his fingertips started tingling. *Come on, Allie.* He looked down at his hand. Was it fading? *Do it*, he willed silently as his arm began tingling as well.

"**Quin**," said Cassius. "**Quintus**."

"No!" Quin burst out, frustration coursing through him as the nausea and tingling passed once more. "Please, Cass, stop."

"Stop what?" Cassius asked, rubbing his head, confusion in his voice. "Quin, are you okay?"

Quin looked up at his friend, but Cassius just stared back at him with wide eyes. Did he really not know what he was doing?

"Stop Calling me," said Quin softly. "Please."

Cassius shook his head. "What?" He leaned forward, frowning. "You look like you're going to pass out. Are you okay? I've been really worried about you. Everyone has."

Quin met Cassius's eyes. He felt raw, and he didn't know who to trust, what to trust.

"You're looking at me like I kicked our ball under Dawn," said Cassius. He was half smiling, but his tone was anguished.

Quin took a breath, trying to steady himself. Cassius was his friend. Had been his friend forever. Was it possible Quin was imagining everything?

"Sorry, Cass," he made himself say. "Just . . . would you mind not saying my name again?"

"O-kayyy," said Cassius confusedly, shaking his head. "It's good to see you, anyway," he said. "Your mother hasn't let anyone up here since you fell ill after the test."

Quin's head was pounding. He had to find a way to get back to Evantra, and to do that, he'd need help. He had to trust someone.

"They decided to delay the induction ceremony until you were better—perks of being Chief Councilor's son." Cassius smiled tentatively at Quin. "Can you believe we're both Callers now? Adriana—your mom said the ceremony will be in a few days, now that you're better."

It felt strange to be reminded of the induction ceremony and his false Calling again. Two days ago it had been the most significant thing in his life.

"Cass," said Quin, sitting up. He would tell Cass what had happened, he decided. That way, if Allie managed to Call Quin back, there would still be someone on Elipsom to carry the truth about Calling. And if she couldn't . . . well, then, he would have someone to make a plan with.

He took a breath. "I haven't been sick," he said. "I was Called to the other side of the planet . . . but it's not a barren wasteland, Cass, it's a continent. Called Evantra."

The grin on Cass's face faded. "Maybe you should lie down," he said, and Quin could hear real concern in his voice.

"I'm fine," said Quin. "I just have to get back to Evantra. They need me. Allie needs me."

"Who is Allie?" said Cassius, frowning.

"A friend," said Quin, resolving to keep her out of it. He could ask for Cass's help without giving up her secrets. "Cass, this is important. Every time we Call, it comes from Evantra. We're stealing, and they're suffering."

Cassius looked down at Quin, his eyes worried.

"Want me to Call you some water?" Cassius reached out his hand.

"No!" cried Quin, knocking Cassius's hand away before he could speak. "Don't you understand? You can't Call. Allie Called me there, Cass. I saw it." He tried to make his friend understand. If Cassius could only *see*.

"Your mom said you'd been having strange dreams. You've been in bed since you collapsed the day of the test, you know that, right?" Cass looked nervous now. "Quin, you haven't *been* anywhere."

Quin leaned back against his pillows. If he couldn't even convince his best friend, how was he going to convince the whole of Orbis? He traced the leaf on his hand, his heart dropping when it didn't pulse in response. His whole body echoed with the loss of Evantra, like he had been more alive there. Here, he was just a shadow of that self.

"Cass, I wasn't dreaming," he tried one more time. "It's why you're not allowed to Call constructed materials—because each piece is unique. Because it exists *before* you Call it. It's not conjuring, it's stealing."

"I don't know, Q," said Cassius, trailing off.

"Fine." Quin gave up. "I think my mother is behind it," he muttered to himself. What could he do if even Cass didn't believe him?

And then he saw Cassius's eyes—and Cassius hesitated. *He knows*, Quin thought—but there was a noise at the door and the moment was lost. Quin looked past Cassius to see Davinia. His heart stopped as she blinked through the gap in the open door, then disappeared from view.

"Dav," Quin rasped, but there was no point. She was already gone.

He knew what she was doing. Running down the stairs, turning onto the landing, and bursting into their mother's room to tell what she had overheard.

And even if she wasn't, it was only a matter of time before she did.

Had he said Allie's name out loud?

Quin steeled himself against the hole he could feel opening inside him. He couldn't let himself think about what it would mean for Allie if they discovered she was a Caller.

And he couldn't spend his time just waiting. For Allie to Call him back to Evantra. For Cassius to believe him.

He had to do something.

CHAPTER SEVENTEEN

Quin was being watched.

He hadn't been alone since he'd woken the morning before. Someone was always with him.

His mother, who asked pointed questions that she thought were subtle. Cassius, who filled every silence. Or Davinia, who still wouldn't meet his eyes.

He wasn't sure who he could trust anymore.

Worst of all, he hadn't felt Allie try to Call him again since the night he arrived. Had she given up on him? He couldn't believe that Allie would give up on anything, at least not willingly. Which brought with it an even worse question: Had something happened to her?

The induction ceremony was planned for the following afternoon. It was as though his time on Evantra had never happened.

And in his more desperate moments, Quin wondered, what if it *hadn't ever* happened? He tried not to let the thought creep in, but as moments shifted past, he could feel it getting harder to prevent. He kept looking for something to cling to, to prove that he hadn't imagined it all. But the mark on his palm just felt like the rest of his hand, and his dreams lay empty.

Still, he felt the absence of the Vine on Elipsom like a dull pain in his chest. It was as though being connected with it on Evantra had awakened something in him. Had uncovered a hole that he hadn't known existed and now couldn't stop seeing.

He needed to find the snippet of vine that had been in his pocket. For some reason, he felt sure he'd be able to know, from that snippet, what was happening with the rest of the Vine.

If the rest of the Vine actually existed at all.

Davinia was at home with him now, sitting at the kitchen table working on tasks their mother had assigned her for the Calling induction ceremony. As well as inducting new Callers, the ceremony would officially announce two new members admitted to Council. Davinia would undoubtedly be one of them.

He still hadn't been able to talk to her about what she'd overheard.

Quin sat down at the table opposite her, watching her sort through papers. He had to at least try and talk to her again before the ceremony. At this point he'd even settle for her bragging, or mocking him.

He waited until she'd found the paper she was looking for, then took a breath.

"Dav . . . ," he said.

She didn't look up.

"Sorry Quin, I really have to concentrate on this," she snapped.

Quin exhaled slowly. Talking and arguing with Davinia had always been a constant in his life. Now that it was gone, he realized how much he had valued it. The silence was stark and unsettling.

"Right. Well, I'm going to the bathroom," said Quin, swallowing his nerves. His mother was out, and with Davinia busy, he at least had a chance to look for the vine. He might not get another one.

"Fine," said Davinia.

Quin walked steadily up the stairs. She'd hear it if he ran.

He paused at the door to his mother's room. Then he took a breath, turned the handle, and pushed it open.

He bypassed her bed and made immediately for her desk. As always, it was completely clear of any clutter, anything personal at all. Quin bent down and pulled open the bottom drawer, which contained a single copy of the Calling charter. He pushed it aside, disgust coating his mouth. He reached farther into the drawer and felt into the back corners, just in case.

Then he froze as he heard footsteps on the stairs.

Heart pounding in his ears, he slid the Calling charter back into place and silently closed the drawer.

He raced to the door, slipping out and clicking it softly closed behind him a moment before Davinia appeared at the top of the stairs.

She locked eyes with him. Quin could feel his heart racing as he looked back at her. "I thought I heard a noise," he blurted, cursing his inability to think of a better excuse.

Davina stared back at him. Quin counted the seconds before she responded.

"Mom's on her way home," she said finally, before turning and walking back downstairs again.

Quin let out the breath he'd been holding. He followed her, then sat back down at the table just as his mother walked through the front door. He'd been so distracted he hadn't even heard her land in the courtyard.

She was holding a set of freshly pressed robes. His grandfather's. "For tomorrow," she said, handing them to him.

Quin almost flinched. He could still picture the Caller on Evantra turning away from Demetrius's crumpled body. He stared at her. His mother raised an eyebrow, and Quin felt a prickle of awareness down the back of his neck that they were playing a game he could only lose. After a beat, he took the robes from her, sliding them as far away from him on the table as he could.

"It's a big day for the Octavius family," she told Quin. "I look forward to seeing you take up the mantle of Caller."

They hadn't even discussed the deception. By the end of the next evening, Quin would officially be a Caller. *The first Caller in history never to have Called a thing,* he thought bitterly. The idea made him sick.

"With you collapsing, we never managed to have our celebration dinner," she continued, her tone mild. "I'd like to do so as a family tonight. And I've invited Cassius along, as a special treat. I thought it might help steady you—you're still not quite yourself."

She left again, her footsteps echoing down the hall. "I'll see you at dinner."

Their mother was late.

Quin had never known her to be late in his life.

He sat at the table with Davinia and Cassius, rubbing his palm and checking the door. A strange weight hung in the air, and Quin didn't know how to dissolve it. There was a gnawing in his chest as he thought of another shared meal, in a cave on Evantra. He wondered whether he'd ever have another meal like it in his life.

Quin almost found himself sighing with relief when Dawn's cry sounded in the courtyard. The sooner they started the meal, the sooner it would be over.

Adriana entered moments later.

"Apologies, all, there was a new development at Chambers."

Quin studied his mother. As usual, her clothes were all gray and immaculate. But there was something slightly off about her, as though her shoes didn't quite match. And beneath her calm tone was a thread of what in anyone else Quin would have described as glee. He felt a bolt of anxiety dart through him.

"I'll just freshen up, and then we can eat," said Adriana. "I've got something new before we have dinner."

She swept out of the room again, and silence fell over the table once more.

"I wonder what happened at Chambers," said Cassius.

Cassius loved knowing what was happening on Council. Even when they were younger, he'd always followed the latest developments, memorizing local measures like other kids obsessed over school gossip.

Quin shifted in his seat, but stopped when he saw Davinia watching him.

When Adriana returned, carrying a steel platter, a sweet, heady scent began to seep into the room, and Quin found himself breathing more deeply as it settled something within him. There was a strange note of familiarity to it.

"Thank you for having me over for dinner, Adria—Ms. Octavius," said Cassius. "This smells delicious."

Quin felt a little like hitting him.

"Thank you, Cassius," said Adriana. "It's a bit of a breakthrough—just a sample of the new stock of food we managed to Call today."

A chill ran though Quin.

"These are called maengoberries," said Adriana with a smile. "You're going to love them. They taste just like ice cream." She placed the platter on the table, then picked up one of the yellow stalks inside. Her knuckles clenched as she snapped off the end.

Quin stopped breathing as she poured the berries onto his plate. He felt as though the floor had been pulled from under him.

The room spun, his vision blurring and heat rushing through his body until he was clammy all over.

Evantra hadn't been a dream.

But even that confirmation did nothing to calm the panic Quin could feel starting to suffocate him.

They'd found the Garden.

The Evantrans had kept it secret for two years. *Two full years.*

And then the moment Quin went there, it had been discovered. It couldn't be a coincidence.

He grasped at his scattered thoughts. Had he said anything since he'd been back? He'd been so careful, he knew he hadn't mentioned the Garden, but . . .

He'd said Allie's name to Cassius.

And Davinia had overheard.

Quin forced his gaze to his sister, but she wouldn't look at him.

Allie.

Was she okay?

Had they captured her?

How could he have been so stupid?!

"You look ill, Quintus," said his mother, her voice etched with concern. "Maybe you should rest before your big day tomorrow."

Quin couldn't look at her. He swallowed, grabbing the table as his vision blurred again, and drove himself to his feet.

He mumbled something incoherent, then staggered from the room, unable to bear being near the sweet scent for a heartbeat longer.

"Don't forget your robes," his mother called. Her heels tapped against the floor after him. Quin stopped, grabbing the doorframe to steady himself as he felt her approach.

He steeled his body, then turned back to face her.

She pushed his grandfather's robes into his arms, and despite the black pit he felt opening up inside him, Quin forced himself to look up. His mother held his gaze, her eyes revealing nothing.

"It's a shame you can't stay for the maengoberries," she said softly to Quin. "I've heard they're delicious."

Quin stepped away from her, beyond caring if she could see his agony.

He pushed himself up the stairs, through his door.

What had they done? What had *he* done?

He threw the robes onto the floor and collapsed on his bed, the soft covers giving little comfort. He felt like his chest had been carved out.

He looked at his hand, which stared dully back at him. *Vine-touched.*

He'd felt such a sense of success when he'd managed to grow something.

But what good was it, anyway? It hadn't helped Evantra. It hadn't helped Allie.

For hours, Quin just lay there. Trying to breathe.

He rolled over, his grandfather's robes mocking him from the floor. He was not a Caller. And for just a fleeting moment, he had been proud of that.

He couldn't let himself believe that Allie wasn't okay. He hated feeling helpless.

There had to be something he could do.

He looked at the robes again, and the desire to throw them out his window streaked through him. If he concentrated hard enough, he could picture red-brown dirt sifting through his fingers. Simply furnished caverns. The smell of damp. And green light, curving through the soil, touching earth with life.

A knock at the door broke his concentration, so soft that he wondered whether he had imagined it.

Quin thought about ignoring it. He didn't want to see his mother, or even Cassius.

But if it was Davinia . . . he wanted to hear her explanation.

"Yeah?" he called out.

When he was met with silence, he went to the door and opened it a fraction, to find there was no one there. He looked down the silent hallway, his gaze catching on something on the floor.

His heart beat faster as he reached down to pick it up.

A jolt went through his fingertips. His hand warmed. And Quin's body flooded with joy and relief and anguish.

The vine.

He stumbled backward into his room, pulling the door shut behind him.

At his touch, it had begun to shimmer with a faint green glow, and Quin almost wept in relief. He moved his fingers along the coil, watching in wonder as the green brightened in response. His fingers caught on a piece of paper curled around the end. Turning on his bedside lamp, he read: *She Called Allie to Chambers.*

Quin's breath caught; his heart pounded in his chest. As though in response to his emotion, the vine grew brighter still, small tendrils beginning to curl at the ends.

He wasn't sure how long he watched it grow, making tiny adjustments to the vine as he thought. As he planned.

As he began to hope again.

CHAPTER
EIGHTEEN

Light had not yet broken the sky when the beat of Dawn's wings woke Quin.

He tucked the vine into his pocket, sitting up to see his mother striding through the courtyard and climbing into the girdle on the rhinodrite's back. With a leap that stole Quin's breath, Dawn vaulted into the dark. Quin watched as their silhouette faded.

He kept watching the sky until he was sure they were gone.

And before light began to filter above the horizon, Quin pulled on clothes, pushed his notebook into his other pocket, and left.

His immediate instinct was to go to Chambers, to try and find Allie before the day began. But there was no guarantee that she'd be alone, and if she wasn't, Quin would lose his chance. There was only one time that day that Quin knew with certainty that his mother would be occupied: in the middle of the induction ceremony.

He questioned his plan again as his feet hit the pavement. There were so many things that could go wrong. But knowing that Allie was at Chambers, at the mercy of his mother . . . A week ago he would have said his mother might be intimidating, but she wasn't bad. But now? He didn't know what to think. All he knew was that he couldn't leave Allie there. She was his friend.

He ran steadily, the sun rising before him. By the time he'd arrived at his destination, it was above the horizon, and Quin was sweating.

He took in deep breaths, wondering again if he was making the right decision.

He paused beside the front door, his gaze automatically pulled to the pot beside it. To the seedlings planted there. For just a breath, he imagined stopping. Reaching out and touching one. Feeling life beneath his fingers. Spending the time to see if he could make it grow.

He had to keep moving, but the plant gave him hope as he raised his hand and knocked on the door.

It was a moment before it was opened by a woman yawning and rubbing sleep from her eyes. She straightened at Quin's appearance and looked over his shoulder, visibly relaxing when she saw there was no one behind him.

"Ms. Valerius," Quin said, bowing his head. "I wondered if I could speak with Zaccheus."

The woman's eyes grew wary.

"He's still in bed," she said. "Best you come back another time."

She didn't bother pretending Zaccheus was her neighbor again. They both knew he was Milo.

"It's okay, Mom." The boy emerged behind her, rested a hand on her shoulder, and then turned to face Quin. "Hello, Quintus."

"Hi, Milo," said Quin.

"You didn't tell your mom who I was," said Milo, studying Quin with bright eyes. "Thanks for that. I mean it."

"It wasn't my name to give," said Quin.

"Are you here to blackmail us?" asked Milo bluntly. "We don't have anything to give you."

Quin shook his head. "No," he said. "I've come with information. And to ask for help, if you'll give it. I didn't know who else to ask."

Milo looked up at his mother, and Quin followed his gaze. Cecelia studied Quin for a moment longer.

"What happens if we take the information and say no to helping?" she asked.

"If you hear me out and say no, I'll leave," Quin promised. "No conditions." If they wouldn't help him, he'd just have to find a different way.

Cecelia opened the door wider, and Quin took a breath and followed her inside.

By the time Quin arrived back at his house, it was almost time to leave again.

He pulled his grandfather's robes over his clothes.

The brown material hung heavy on his shoulders, falling from his arms in thick folds that dragged on the floor when he moved. Quin's skin felt clammy all over, and he almost recoiled as he caught sight of himself in the mirror.

His hair stood up at all angles. He pushed it down until it was almost in his eyes, knowing that if he didn't fix it, his mother would later.

His eyes were grave as he studied himself in the glass. He looked like a Caller.

He hadn't wanted to wear the robes. Had thought about leaving them behind. But if he left the house without them, it would raise suspicion. And right now, he couldn't afford to set a foot out of place.

The vine was tucked into his pocket, both ends curling with small leaves that hadn't been there the night before.

He could hear noise downstairs and knew he couldn't delay any longer. Quin steeled himself. It would be his first interaction with Davinia since the maengoberries at dinner. He had hoped she would already be at Chambers.

But when Quin reached the bottom of the staircase it was to find Cassius, shuffling his feet in the otherwise empty marble foyer.

"Quin!" said Cassius, relief and tension somehow both clear in his voice. "Your mom asked if I'd make the journey to Chambers with you. She was worried you might still be feeling sick."

Crap! Quin forced a smile at his friend. "I'll be glad for the company," he lied.

Cassius smiled back at him, and for an instant Quin imagined what it would be like if he had actually passed the Calling test. If he'd never been to Evantra. If he and Cassius were still the Quin and Cass who played in the hallways of Chambers together, who had no secrets from each other.

They walked in silence to the vehicle, and Cassius paused beside it to let Quin in first.

Rather than argue, Quin just slid inside with a nod of thanks as the door clicked shut behind them.

He watched the boxed trees flick past out the window, a cold chill settling over him. Part of him hoped that Cassius was the one who had left the vine and the note, but Quin couldn't even ask him, in case he wasn't.

Cassius cleared his throat. "Are you . . . okay? You know, after the other day?" He didn't wait for Quin to respond. "You do seem much better this morning."

Quin smiled tightly back at him. "I'm fine, Cass," he said, but his mind was on how he was going to make sure Milo was ready while Cassius was around. They'd all gone to the same school; Cassius would recognize Milo immediately. He'd have to find a way to get away from his friend.

They soon arrived at Chambers and walked through the main doors, the foyer buzzing with activity as people arrived for the ceremony.

Quin's eyes flicked around for Milo, but he couldn't see him anywhere. Quin paused. Cassius stopped and looked at him.

"Oh, shoot," said Quin, feeling desperate. "I told my mom I'd get something from her office for her before the ceremony." It was a poor excuse, and the words caught on his tongue.

"What was it?" asked Cassius. Quin froze. He hadn't really expected Cassius to question him.

"Just some notes," Quin said, wondering if Cassius could hear the catch in his voice. "For her speech."

Cassius met his eyes, and Quin saw a flash of something passing through them—something that told him everything he needed to know.

"Oh, those," said Cassius, looking away as he spoke. "She's already got them."

In someone else it might have been a genuine response. But Quin knew Cassius; he knew what it looked like when he lied. His mother had sent Cassius to keep an eye on Quin. To make sure he went to the ceremony. *Because Cassius had told his mother about Allie.* Now Cassius's eyes were down, and he was smoothing his hair and clearing his throat.

Quin felt like he'd been punched in the stomach.

"It was you," Quin breathed, unable to stop the words from tripping off his tongue. "*You* told her about Allie."

Cassius looked up, his face pained. He offered no denial.

"Do you have any idea what you've done?" said Quin, anger burning inside him.

"On Council I can make a real difference. I can mean something," Cassius pleaded. Quin just stared as Cassius took a step toward him. "Your mother wants what's best for us, Quin. Next year we can make sure you get on, and then you can effect change, too."

Quin shook his head and took a step back. His friend had betrayed him for a place on Council. And the worst part was, Cass really believed in what he was saying.

"I'm not . . . ," Quin started to say, but he halted when footsteps echoed across the foyer toward them.

"Quintus. Cassius. I was starting to worry you'd both gotten lost on your way here." Adriana approached, a Council member on either side of her.

"Hello, Ms. Octavius," said Cassius, turning to address Quin's mother. "We were just on our way in."

Quin could feel the heat of his mother's gaze on him. He wouldn't be able to get away to check while she was there. Quin would just have to trust that everything was ready.

"We're all so thrilled about today's ceremony," said Adriana, still watching Quin. "Let's move into the Central Chamber, shall we? We don't want to be late."

His mother turned and started walking. The other Council members waited until Quin and Cassius followed, one of them falling into step beside Quin.

"How are you feeling?" she asked kindly. Quin looked up to see the woman who had tested him. She smiled at Quin. "I must admit, it was such an honor to be part of your test," she continued. "I look forward to seeing what is in store for you in the future, Quintus. I know we're going to see great things."

Quin grimaced at her, unable to muster a real smile. Hopefully she'd put it down to nerves.

She fell silent as they reached the ornate wooden doors that led to the Central Chamber. Quin had always loved the intricacy and detail of the patterning. Curves swirled up each side, twisting across the panels to meet at the top. Now, Quin wondered sourly whether they'd been made on Elipsom hundreds of years ago or just Called from Evantra.

Adriana pushed the doors, which slowly creaked open to reveal the Central Chamber. The interior was larger than Quin's whole house, and no matter how many times he entered, he was always taken aback by it. The ceilings were almost as tall as the building itself—the Central Chamber was the only room in the whole of Chambers to use the full height—and from the grand doors, tiers of seating led gradually down to a dais.

The seats were already a quarter filled, and Quin focused on breathing as the people who were seated turned around to study them.

Adriana smiled politely as they walked down the wide center aisle, shaking a few hands and regally inclining her head. She would never be so gauche as to admit it, but she loved her role as Chief Councilor.

They reached the dais, where nine others Quin's age were already seated. That was it for the year. Ten new Callers in all of Evantra. Eleven, if you included Quin.

The rest of the Callers were sitting quietly, their bodies tense with barely concealed excitement. As Quin passed the front row, he could see proud family members waving. He felt his gut turn. These people were relying on stolen goods. But who could blame them if it was all they had? Becoming a Caller was a mark of status. Some came from as far out as the Kolandra ranges and the Lee Islands, and if these new Callers were the first in generations, it would change the lives of whole communities.

One of the new Callers was silently Calling what looked like grains of soil to the palm of his hand. Quin watched, fascinated, as the pile in the center of his hand grew speck by speck.

The boy looked up as they approached the dais and blushed, blowing away the grains of dust.

"Chief Councilor," he stammered. "Sorry, I . . ."

Adriana smiled warmly at the boy. "It is natural to want to practice your gift," she said. "I look forward to seeing your confidence grow as you Call bigger things."

The boy blushed again. It was always difficult to tell whether Adriana's words were meant as a compliment or an insult.

She took her seat on the dais, gesturing for Quin and Cassius to sit beside her.

Quin sat, overcome with a deep wave of longing. Where on Evantra had the soil come from? Had it touched the vine? He clenched his hands together in his lap to stop from reaching out and picking up one of the grains.

The chamber slowly filled with people. Quin sat silently, frustration rubbing beneath his skin. He was desperate to leave, to act, to get away from his mother. The wait was almost unbearable. He could feel Adriana watching him between her conversations with people who approached the dais. The buzz of noise made his head ache.

Finally, Adriana stood, and a hush fell over the room.

The ceremony was about to begin.

CHAPTER
NINETEEN

Adriana walked to the center of the dais.

"To Call is to create," she said, her voice solemn. "It is the basis of our very existence. When we had nothing, it was Calling that ensured Elipsom was provided for. The ability to will things into being is not one that we take lightly.

"**Wind**," she Called.

The audience gasped as a gust of wind swept through the chamber, rattling the wooden door.

"**Fire**," she Called next, her voice ringing out through the chamber.

The front of the stage lit up, flames licking toward the front row. Adriana watched silently as people scrambled from their seats.

"**Water**," she Called, raising her hands and dousing the flames.

As the last ember died, there was silence. And then darkness descended over the room.

"**Light**," Adriana Called finally.

She held her hand aloft, and daylight illuminated the wall behind her. The crowd gasped again.

Quin wondered where in Evantra the light had been pulled from. What had been left in darkness.

He looked out into the chamber, where everyone seemed to be staring at the wall. Quin turned around to see the Calling Principles etched in the center of the light.

> *We Call to serve all of Elipsom*
> *We do not Call for ourselves*
>
> *We Call no more than we need*
> *We do not waste what is Called*
>
> *We Call for the benefit of the community*
> *We do not Call for selfish gain*
>
> *We Call things in their purest form*
> *We do not Call what is constructed*

A spark of anger burned beneath Quin's skin. The Calling Principles had always sounded so grand and noble—and yet they were designed entirely to support a deception.

Elipsomians deserved to know that things were Called from *somewhere*. If everything was laid bare, there might even be a way the two continents could work together.

Adriana Called more light into the room, and the Principles slowly faded from the wall.

Quin flashed back to Allie's face when he'd told her that Calling was willing things into being. She would have hated Adriana's display. The thought bolstered him, and Quin sat up straighter as he watched his mother. He would not be intimidated by her.

"The position of Caller is one of both leader and servant. This year, we induct eleven new servants to the hallowed rank, and admit two new members to Council."

Adriana looked back to the dais, frowning slightly at the empty seat at the end of the row. Quin looked out into the crowd, then back to the seat. Davinia still hadn't arrived.

"As Callers, we are bound by the principles outlined in our charter. Today, we vow together to adhere to them."

"The first Caller to be inducted is Linus Justus. Linus, would you please step forward."

The boy who had been Calling soil stepped forward, his head down and face red.

Quin could see a woman in the front row sitting on the edge of her seat. Life would be different for them when they went home, that was etched all over Mrs. Justus's face. They would be considered people of significance.

"Thank you, Linus," said Adriana. "Linus, do you vow to serve the community and uphold the Calling Principles?"

"I do," said Linus quietly. His head darted up, then quickly back down again, his ears flushing as red as his face as the audience whooped.

"Linus Justus, I admit you to the rank of Caller," said Adriana.

She bent down and fastened the silver band around his wrist that would mark him as Caller, and he darted back to his seat, half bowing on the way.

"The next person to be inducted is Cassius Servius," said Adriana. "Cassius, would you please step forward."

Cassius stood and approached Adriana. She smiled at him as genuinely as Quin had ever seen her smile, and Quin clenched his jaw. Even knowing the truth about all his mother had done, he couldn't help but envy the real affection she clearly had for his best friend.

"As well as being named Caller today, Cassius also becomes the youngest person ever to be admitted to Council," said Adriana.

Applause filled the chamber. *People love to witness history*, thought Quin. Well, he hoped they were ready.

"Cassius, do you vow to serve the community and uphold the Calling Principles?"

"I do," said Cassius.

"Cassius Servius, I admit you to the rank of Caller," said Adriana. He smiled humbly as Adriana clasped a Caller's band around his wrist.

When she was finished, Cassius turned to the crowd.

"**Flowers**," he Called, opening his palms to catch them, then throwing them out to the delighted audience members.

Quin felt like he was going to be sick.

Adriana brought forward and inducted the other new Callers, until only Quin remained.

He tried not to fidget in his seat. Where *was* Milo?

"Finally, it is my utmost pleasure to be welcoming another Octavius to the rank of Caller today," Adriana said, locking eyes with Quin. "My own son, Quintus Octavius."

Quin could feel the audience turn to look at him. He met his mother's eyes. Read the threat in them. And the triumph.

Quin stood, walking slowly to join her at the front of the dais. If Milo didn't show up, he was just going to have to run and hope.

He looked out at the crowd watching. There were hundreds of people in the chamber.

Adriana waited until Quin was standing directly before her, held out her hand to shake his, and—

"It's a lie!" a voice shouted from the back of the auditorium, and Quin inwardly breathed a sigh of relief at the sight of curly black hair.

Adriana's head snapped up.

"Calling is stealing," Milo continued loudly. "It is taking things from somewhere else."

Adriana motioned to the guard force, who were already steadily weaving their way to the back of the auditorium.

"Nothing comes from nothing," yelled Milo. And at his words, twenty others from the Spurges stood to their feet beside him and took up the chant.

"Nothing comes from nothing! Nothing comes from nothing!"

Adriana took a step forward, and Quin seized the moment. He ran.

He pushed his way down the side of the hall, past the people standing and craning their necks to look at what was happening.

Quin moved faster, his focus shifting forward to the door, wondering how he was going to get through without people noticing. The sight of Milo fighting off one of the guards stopped him in his tracks. But when Milo looked over and met his eyes, Quin felt his friend's determination cut through the air.

"This is my choice," he heard the other boy say loudly. "My name is Milo Valerius. I can Call and I *choose* not to." He looked back at Quin.

Quin swallowed. Heart heavy, he nodded once at Milo, then turned for the door.

Behind him, his mother was already taking control of the riot in the auditorium. Quickly, Quin tried the handle. It was locked, and his stomach sank. Time for plan B.

He reached down into his pocket and pulled out the vine, his hand steady. And as he did, a faint green glow began to dance across the floor.

Breath shaking, Quin pressed his hand and the vine to the door, hoping that he wasn't wrong.

For a horrible instant, nothing happened. And then, slowly, the green light wrapping its way through the pattern grew stronger.

Quin took a breath and focused on the door. He had a feeling that his connection to the vine was emotional as much as it was physical and mental. The more strongly he felt, the more responsive the vine was.

He imagined the tree that the door once was. He felt his heart physically aching for the loss of its life.

There were no living roots to grasp, no living vine to pull them toward. So Quin focused on the grains of wood and, pushing into the door with his mind, he pulled them toward the vine in his hand.

The door began to tremble beneath his fingers. Quin poured himself into it, and with a final creak it began to splinter, like a branch being split beyond breaking point.

Shards of wood rained down on him, until suddenly, there was a hole large enough for Quin to climb through.

He thanked Milo silently again as the boy let out a shout that Quin suspected was to keep attention away from the splintering door.

He glanced back to see his mother directing guards, and his heart stopped as she looked up and saw him.

She would have to choose between pursuing Quin and maintaining order in the auditorium. Quin was hoping he knew which she'd pick, but he wasn't going to stay to find out.

With a final look at the door, Quin turned and started racing back toward the central foyer. He had no idea where Allie would be within the maze of Chambers, but he figured that his mother's office was the best place to start looking. He rounded the corner into the foyer and started toward the hallway that would lead him to Adriana's office.

Only to come to a complete stop when Davinia blocked his path.

CHAPTER TWENTY

Quin readjusted his grip on the vine, wrapping it between his fingers.

Davinia's eyes flicked down to Quin's hand, then back to his face, her expression unreadable.

"You have to listen to me, Dav," Quin said, taking a step forward. "The other side of our planet *isn't* barren. Every time we Call something, it comes from there. I went there. I wasn't sick—I was in a place called Evantra. A place we're destroying."

Davinia rolled her eyes.

"You're getting to be almost as dramatic as Mom," she said. Then, more quietly she added, "I know, Quin. I'm the one who left you that plant. And the note."

Quin felt something settle inside him. Relief, at having his sister back. He took another step toward her.

"Have you seen Allie?" he whispered. "Is she okay? How did Mom know about . . . everything?"

Davinia sighed. "After you disappeared . . . she went through your room. She took your notebook. At first we thought you'd just run away to process everything about . . . the test." She swallowed, and Quin saw the guilt flash across her face. "But then your old notebook disappeared right while Mom was looking at it. She Called you back almost as soon as she figured out where you were. Although it didn't work the first time." She frowned. "She didn't know why."

They'd been in the caves then, Quin realized. It must have been when he'd been touching the Vine.

"After that . . . well, they were hardly going to leave a Caller on Evantra. Allie almost got you back a few times before Council learned her full name and Called her here to stop her from doing more. But until then, Mom made Cassius and me Call you if we saw you fading. To hold you here."

He'd suspected as much, but it still hurt to have it confirmed.

"They're holding her at the end of the western corridor," said Davinia. "You can't miss it, there's a guard posted outside the doorway." She looked over Quin's shoulder. "You should go."

There was hesitation in her voice, though, and Quin took another step toward her. His feet itched to start running, but he sensed that this moment was important. Something was in the balance.

"Are you okay?" he asked her.

He could see from the look in Davinia's eye that she was about to brush him off.

"Dav?" he said.

She sighed. "You're not from here, Quin," she said bluntly. "You're from Evantra." Her eyes went to his hand again. "It's why you've got that weird birthmark. Sorry to have to be the one to tell you, and like this, but—it seems like the thing you need to know right now."

Quin blinked back at her. He almost laughed, a sob catching in the back of his throat. He had missed his sister.

"How is that possible?" he asked her.

Davinia looked back over his shoulder again. "How long have we got?" she asked.

"Not long," said Quin, looking back over his shoulder. "You want to help with that?"

Davinia grinned, a flicker of her usual spark flashing in her eyes.

"**Rock**," she Called.

Quin jumped as a boulder thudded to the ground behind him, blocking the hallway he'd just come through.

"Did you really need to Call a *boulder*?" he said.

Davinia shrugged. "I figure Evantra will probably forgive me if I help get you back to them."

She took a breath, her shoulders trembling slightly, and Quin realized just how unsteady she was.

"She took you," said Davinia, shaking her head as though she still couldn't quite believe it. Quin opened his mouth to defend Allie, but closed it when he realized what she was saying. She was talking about his own mother.

"When you were a baby. Mom took you from Evantra."

"What?" he said, unable to process her words.

"That mark," said Davinia, gesturing to his hand. "And apparently the fact that you can make plants grow." She gave Quin a look. He couldn't even bring himself to respond.

"Having you close to her makes the connection to Evantra stronger," said Davinia. "It makes Callers around you stronger. It's why Octaviuses for generations have all had the gift: because our family has been Calling babies and covering it up for years." Her eyes were serious, and her words were bitter. "Mom told me, after I passed my test. She said it was a condition of my being on Council, that I support our legacy. There are only a few Councilors who know. Apparently I'm one of the lucky ones," she added bitterly. "It's disgusting." She closed her eyes and shook her head. "And yet, I am selfishly glad that it meant I got a brother. I got you."

She looked up and met Quin's eyes, and he could see tears in hers.

The Octavius legacy was a lie, too.

Quin felt like he might collapse.

Davinia watched him.

"You don't have time to freak out, little brother," she said. "You have to get Allie, and you have to get out of here. Go back to Evantra. Our mother was the only one strong enough to Call you and Allie here, but who knows if she can do it again. I know even keeping you here was a strain for Cassius."

"I don't know how to get there," said Quin, swallowing the tremble in his voice.

Davinia raised her eyebrows at him. "You got this far," she said.

Shouts echoed down the hallway. Quin turned around and looked at the boulder Davinia had Called. It wouldn't hold their mother long, either.

"Go," said Davinia. "I'll try and stall her."

Quin hesitated. "There's a boy from the Spurges. Milo. He helped me today. Can you . . . look after him?"

Davinia raised her eyebrows, but she nodded.

"I love you, Dav," Quin said.

Davinia wiped her face. "Get out of here," she said.

Quin took a breath. The voices were getting louder.

"Quin," Davinia called, and he looked over his shoulder. "I love you too."

Quin paused and smiled. Then he ran.

He rounded the corner, unable to stop a chuckle as he heard Davinia yelling that he'd run for the main exit, and she'd unsuccessfully tried to stop him with the boulder.

Only Dav.

He kept running, sprinting down the corridor that stretched alongside the massive open courtyard at the center of Chambers.

Out of the corner of his eye Quin could see Dawn, standing between two platforms. It seemed to him that her head was tracking his movement, and for a heartbeat part of him was tempted to run out into the courtyard and over to her. But not yet.

He pushed himself faster and harder as he neared the western corridor, pausing before he turned the next corner, catching his breath. Slowly, he looked around the corner—then quickly jerked back. The guard Davinia had warned him about was right there.

Inhaling slowly, he steadied himself. He had no real weapon, and no idea what he was doing. The only thing he had was the element of surprise.

So he would use it.

He held tight to the vine, took another breath, and then burst around the corner, pushing his grief and determination into the vine, willing light to it and closing his eyes.

He heard the man cry out as a bright-green flash filled the corridor. Quin opened his eyes and ran, hoping that a moment would be enough.

Quin rushed at the guard, hearing his gasp of surprise as Quin grabbed at his waist. The guard kicked back at Quin's legs reflexively, automatically responding to an unknown threat. A sharp pain shot through Quin's leg as the guard's foot connected, but Quin could think of only one thing: the lumina ballista he snatched from the man's holster.

CHAPTER
TWENTY-ONE

Fumbling, Quin checked the switch at the top of the ballista that controlled pulse direction, hoping that his memory was accurate.

The guard stumbled to his feet as the green light faded. He took a step toward Quin, arm outstretched.

Quin flicked the switch, sinking to his knees in relief as the yellow light flashed and the guard crumpled to the ground.

Quin forced himself to his feet again, stumbling over to check on him. When he was sure the guard was breathing steadily, Quin unclasped the security band from around the man's wrist. His hands shook as he snapped it onto his own.

He held the security band to the pad on the door, finally exhaling when he heard the lock click.

With another breath, he pushed the door open.

Allie was staring back at him, her eyes wide.

She was sitting on a metallic bed in the corner—the only furniture in the room. Natural light filtered through a closed window and bounced off shiny walls, and Quin could see that her hands had been bound and her mouth gagged. She looked otherwise uninjured, though, and Quin let out the breath he hadn't realized he was holding. "*Allie.*"

He strode over to her and bent down, untying the silver cloth they'd used to gag her.

"Quin," she whispered, her eyes filling with tears. "I tried to Call you back, but it didn't work. And then guards came to our cave. Quin, they found the tunnels, and then everything went black and I haven't been able to Call anything from in here and there was nothing I could *do.*" She started weeping in earnest, and Quin felt pricks of heat at the back of his own eyes. It was the first time he'd seen her so discomposed. He sat down on the bed beside her.

"I'm so sorry, Allie," he said, wishing he had more to offer but knowing that they were short on time. "I'm so glad you're all right." Hesitantly, he placed his hand on her shoulder.

"I'm going to take your wrist cuffs off," he told her gently, and at her nod, he reached behind her back and held the guard's band to the cuffs. With a soft *snick*, they fell to the floor, and Allie wrapped her arms around him, burying her face into his shoulder.

Quin held her, giving her a moment to breathe. *Taking* a moment to breathe.

When her sobbing had subsided, he let go.

"We need to get out of here before Adriana discovers us," he said softly. There wasn't time to talk, to process everything that had happened. That would come later. "Can you walk?"

He watched Allie gather herself, dashing away tears and looking at him with steely resolve, despite the red rings around her eyes. "I can walk," she told him.

Quin stood, helping her up behind him. He peered out the door, relieved to see that apart from the unconscious guard, the corridor was clear.

His leg aching from where he'd been kicked, he pulled them along as quickly as he could manage, mindful that Allie was likely still stiff, too. Her gaze darted around the corridor, her breath shaky, and Quin realized that the room they had just left might have been all she had seen of Chambers. All she had seen of Elipsom. He wished he could show her the good parts, too.

She glanced down at the guard as they passed, then looked back up at Quin, a question in her eyes.

"I'll tell you later," he said.

They half walked, half ran down the corridor, heading for the central courtyard. For the first time that day, Quin let himself believe that they might make it. That they might find a way back to Evantra.

He led Allie to the side entrance, his heart swelling at the sight of Dawn pawing the ground between her mounting blocks.

Allie stopped suddenly. "Is that a rhinodrite?" she asked.

Quin paused beside her, feeling strangely nervous about sharing his plan.

"I thought . . . since you said on Evantra anyone can ride them, I thought maybe she was our best way out of here."

Allie turned to meet his eyes, and Quin smiled at the spark in hers. "Let's try it," she said.

"It could go terribly," Quin warned her. "I've never ridden one before."

"Neither have I," said Allie. She crooked a smile back at him. "I can always Call us a lot of pillows if things go horribly wrong."

Quin choked on a laugh. Then he took a breath and nodded, and together they ran into the courtyard.

Dawn's eyes were on them, and Quin found himself speeding up, running toward her. Along one side of the courtyard he could see the huge stone wall at the back of the Central Chamber. He tried not to think about where his mother might be, what she was doing.

His chest started to burn. His leg throbbed. But Allie was running right alongside him, her face determined.

Ignoring all advice he'd ever been given, they ran straight toward Dawn, their footsteps echoing softly against the stone.

He slowed himself as they neared the rhinodrite, and Allie followed suit. Dawn studied them, her large brown eyes meeting Quin's. There was a chain around one of her legs, Quin realized as they got closer. He had never gotten close enough to see that she was bound in place.

Now, Quin reached out his hand. He approached the rhinodrite slowly, hoping that his mother had been lying about their aggression.

His heart beat faster, but he couldn't rush. Not this.

"I'm going to try and take the chain off," he whispered. He didn't know if rhinodrites understood language, but he spoke aloud just in case, and Dawn remained still and silent. The heat of her rough skin warmed his. He held his wristband to the lock on her chains, but wasn't surprised when they didn't fall off. His mother's band would be the only one keyed to it.

He glanced over at Allie, who was watching him calmly. Trusting him.

Gripping the vine in his hand, he thought about the joy of finding Allie. He poured his happiness into the plant. A new shoot started taking shape at the end of the vine, and he fed it into the lock on the chain. Then he willed it to grow fuller and larger until, with a clink, the lock burst open.

As it did, the vine touched Dawn's leg, sending a green glow spiraling up under her thick skin. He heard Allie gasp, then backed up until he was face-to-face with Dawn.

She bent her head down toward him and Quin braced himself. But no impact came, and when Quin looked up, it was to see her blinking back at him.

Hesitantly, he reached his hand out. He held his breath as Dawn folded her body onto all fours.

"We need you to take us away from here," whispered Quin.

Dawn held his gaze a moment. Then she pressed her head to his hand.

Quin's vision blurred.

CHAPTER
TWENTY-TWO

He saw the planet from above.

Not as he knew it, but as it once must have been.

Shades of green wove and knit together across the entire surface. Quin was aware that his body was still in the courtyard, but he could smell fresh leaves. Could feel the crispness of the air. Where shiny buildings and mines now dotted Elipsom . . . there were trees. Dark forests met emerald-green hills and thickets of shrubs that burst from the ground. Vines of different shapes and thicknesses traversed the planet, hanging between trees, then rejoining the earth. Quin could see it, *feel* it, pulsing with vibrant life. And through the center of this world ran the Vine.

He felt Allie take his hand beside him. Heard her intake of breath as she saw what he did.

And he wondered. Whether more than just Evantra could be healed after all.

He would come back, he vowed. After he'd healed the Vine on Evantra, he'd come back to Elipsom. He would see what could be restored.

He closed his eyes, breathing deeply. And when he opened them again, he was back with Dawn in the courtyard once more.

They had to leave. His mother would catch up with them soon. But as he gazed at Dawn, Quin felt a peace pass through him.

She bowed her head before him. When Quin hesitated, she nudged him gently, her head sending warmth spreading through his body.

"Can you climb up?" he asked Allie, turning to face her for the first time and dropping her hand quickly.

Allie nodded, determination written in her frame. She clambered up, gently stroking Dawn's neck, then scooted aside to make room for Quin.

Quin touched Dawn's head, and then, satisfied that she was okay, he climbed the platform and swung his leg up over her back.

"Are you ready?" he whispered. Allie wrapped her arms around him.

He braced himself, then rested his hands against the sides of Dawn's head, his palm burning with heat and joy as he did.

Dawn crouched, ready for takeoff, when his mother's voice echoed into the courtyard.

Quin looked up to see her striding outside, Davinia on one side of her and Cassius on the other. Just behind them was the woman from Quin's test.

"**Quintus Octavius**," Adriana said, and Quin felt a strange shiver run through him. His mother was clearly trying to Call him, but why would she be trying to hold him on Elipsom when there was no one Calling him on the other side?

Just past her, at the entrance to the courtyard, Quin could see half a dozen members of the Elipsom guard force.

Inside there seemed to be several of the new Callers and their families watching on with interest.

"You need to get down," Adriana said calmly. But Quin could hear the steel and urgency in her tone. "You're not well, Quin, and that girl with you is dangerous," she said. "Let us help you."

Quin met her eyes. Forced her to see the determination in his.

"You are a liar, and a thief," he said, his voice even. "You've let people believe that Calling is a right and a responsibility. But it comes from greed and selfishness. Calling is a lie based on lies. I will not be part of it."

Dawn tensed, lowering her horn toward the Callers.

Quin ignored Cassius, who had made his allegiance clear, and didn't look at Davinia. He wouldn't betray her by acknowledging her.

He spoke instead to the Caller behind his mother, raising his voice so that the people inside might hear him as well.

"The people from the Spurges are right," he told them. "Nothing comes from nothing. When we Call, it *does* come from something. It comes from another place—Evantra, the continent on the other side of the planet.

"I don't know if you knew about Evantra. But you should know. You should find out. Because we are stealing from them, destroying their land. One day, there will be nothing left to take from Evantra, and then we'll have lost everything. I believe that there is another way forward, if we choose to live differently.

"I promise to come back and help," he continued, allowing himself one look at his sister. "But first I have to save the place we've been ruining for far too long."

Then he leaned down and whispered, "Let's go, Dawn."

Dawn rocked back, then sprang into the air, swinging her wings wide.

For breathless moments, they were free. Wind rushed through Quin's hair, biting his cheeks and filling his chest.

"Where are we going?" Allie called into his ear.

"I was planning to fly north," Quin said, "to the Lee Islands, on the edge of Elipsom. I want to see how far Dawn can travel. If she can make that distance, she might be able to get us all the way to Evantra."

Dawn wheeled higher into the air, as if she knew what he was saying.

But then she cried out in pain, and Quin looked across to see fire at the tip of her wing.

He looked down at his mother. Her hand was raised toward them.

Allie shifted behind him, reaching out her own hand.

"**Water**." He heard her whispered Call catch on the

wind as the sky above Dawn's wing opened and liquid doused the flames.

His mother reached out her hand, and Quin felt Dawn falter as rocks began raining from the sky. Quin pressed closer to her, stroking her head and coaxing her forward.

They flew through to the other side of the rockfall and had a moment of respite. They just had to get out of Adriana's sight line.

Quin's head spun. He couldn't stop thinking about her Calling him back in the courtyard. Why would she do that, unless there was a way for them to leave?

He nudged Dawn forward, urging her on as a yellow beam flashed from the ground.

His mother had a lumina ballista. And she had sent a pulse wave at them.

And looking down at her, at the woman who knew the truth and *chose* to continue committing crimes against Evantra, Quin realized—he didn't really know her at all.

She wasn't his mother. She had lied to him his entire life. She had used him since he was born. And she hadn't even hesitated to Call a ballista to get what she wanted.

Quin felt the fury that had been sitting beneath his skin spill out from him and into the vine he clutched.

He saw layers of green. Patterns. He thought about Adriana Calling his name, and about *how* things traveled from Evantra.

"Allie," yelled Quin, resolve stealing through him. He held tight to the vine, wrapping one end around his hand and giving the other end to Allie. "Try Calling home."

Allie didn't hesitate; she wrapped the vine around her hand and then held fast to it. Like she trusted him without reservation.

"You think my Calling and your Vine-Touchedness will work together? We need a better name for that," she added in the same breath.

"Yes. I think . . . ," Quin began as light pierced the sky once more. "I think that if you Call Evantra, my connection to the Vine will pull us there."

"Are you just sensing it?" asked Allie.

"I hope so," said Quin, a strange lightness washing through him at the words.

Allie laughed. Quin felt her lean forward, closer to him.

"**Evantra**," she Called.

Quin felt the vine around his wrist burn, then erupt into green light.

He heard Allie exclaim and Dawn cry with triumph as she beat her wings once, twice . . .

And then the blinding green exploded into white, and Quin could no longer see anything.

He felt Dawn, sure and steady beneath him, her wings stretched wide. He felt Allie behind him, arms clenched around his waist.

Heat danced across his skin, burning hotter and brighter until he couldn't bear it. His ears were ringing and his head was pounding and he felt like he was going to explode.

And then there was green again. Soft, this time, chasing the burn away.

It shifted and changed and was somehow all the greens at once. And then Quin started to see familiar patterns. The layers of the Vine.

They fell deeper through the patterns, but it was as though Allie's Call was tethering them, pulling them forward.

Time slowed. Quin reached out, his hand indistin-guishable from the air.

Streaks in other colors dashed past them, prisms of darkness against the green glow.

Were those *things being Called*?

Quin felt himself breathe. He felt like he *was* a breath.

Still, Dawn kept going.

Another bright flash of white flared, quickly followed by a burst of green.

And with a loud cry, Dawn suddenly pushed upward.

Quin's vision danced.

As it gradually cleared, his heart almost stopped.

They were in the sky above Evantra.

Above the fields that he'd walked in two days before.

They had somehow traveled through the Vine. *Through the world.*

Dawn swooped downward, her call echoing through the late-afternoon sky.

Quin blinked as he took in the sprawling landscape beneath them. He could feel a steady pulse running through his hand.

His heart ached as they looked over Evantra. He could see Allie's cave. The rocks where they'd entered to find the Vine underground. More than anything, he wanted to touch the soil. To hold a handful of it.

He could hear Allie's ragged breathing behind him. Felt her laugh in disbelief.

"Quin. Quin, we're home."

Quin clung to Dawn, his legs and heart aching.

He grasped the length of vine, using his fading energy to pull it into two pieces, one around his wrist and the other around Allie's.

"Keep it around bare skin," he told her, as he tied the other off around his wrist. He was too tired to explain that it should anchor them, that his mother hadn't been able to Call him when he was touching it.

There was so much to do. Find somewhere to land, and find their friends. Heal Evantra. Heal it all, if he could.

He didn't think Adriana would stop coming after them.

Quin heard Allie whisper something behind him, and a second later she handed him a pillow.

He laughed until he had tears in his eyes.

And when he leaned forward and touched Dawn's head, when he tugged the vine around his wrist, it pulsed in response. Quin felt a coil of warmth wrap its way through him.

Allie was right.

They were home.

ᴬCKNOWLEDGMENTS

I am grateful to so many incredible people for the way that this book has turned out.

To my editor, Taylor Norman: Gosh, I have had such a great time working on this with you. Thank you for everything.

Massive thanks to Lydia Ortiz for designing everything inside and out, and to Kaley McKean for bringing Quin (and the Vinc!) to life on this cover.

To my amazing parents, Sally and Paul, who encouraged me to come back to this book.

To all my friends and family who read early drafts; especially to Zoe, Heather, Jade, Edwina, Zanni, and Eve.

And to Luke, Eli, Eva, and Mae: I am so lucky to share this with you.